The Wooden
People

The Wooden People

by

Myra Paperny

Illustrated by Ken Stampnick

Little, Brown and Company/Boston/Toronto

FIRST EDITION

T 10/76

Library of Congress Cataloging in Publication Data

Paperny, Myra.
   The wooden people.

   SUMMARY: A young boy, angry because his family is
moving again, begins to play with puppets rather than
make new friends.
   [1. Puppets and puppet-plays—Fiction.   2. Family
life—Fiction]   I. Title.
PZ7.P2Wo   [Fic]   76–24816
ISBN 0–316–69040–6

Designed by D. Christine Benders

Published simultaneously in Canada
by Little, Brown & Company (Canada) Limited

PRINTED IN THE UNITED STATES OF AMERICA

In memory of my mother
Jessie Green
who knew the truth of
childhood

Contents

The Wooden People

I

Teddy Launches
More Than a Boat

"MAMA, MAMA, COME QUICK, the boathouse is finally ready," Lisa Stein shrieked as she ran up the steps, across the broad veranda and into their big white house. "Mama, where are you?"

Lisa dashed down the long front hall, past the living room with its closed French doors, and into the kitchen where Mama usually could be found. In the spacious kitchen she saw Mama's pan of dough sitting under a cloth on the wooden table. The rolling pin rested beside the balloon of creamy dough but there was no Mama in sight.

"That's strange," she murmured to no one in particular. Lisa paused a moment to lick her finger and dip it into the measuring cup of sugar and cinnamon that rested on the oilcloth cover. Then, shaking her long straight black hair out of her eyes, she headed for the walk-in pantry. Only the neat rows of labeled jars and bottles of preserved fruit and vegetables greeted her. Slowly she left the room but, moving down the hall, her pace again increased as she climbed the stairs to the bedrooms.

"Well, where is she?" came a voice from below. Having searched all the bedrooms, Lisa looked over the curving banister which all of the four young Steins loved to slide down. She gave a snort of puzzlement. Her brother Teddy waited below in the hall. His hair was the same brunette color as hers but it was curly. His face was tanned a dark bronze color from the sun and wind on the lake. At twelve he was a year younger than Lisa, but people often mistook them for twins.

"Come on then, Lisa. All the kids are waiting for us to launch the boat."

"But we can't launch it until Mama gives it a final inspection. Remember we promised her when we started building the boat that it would be seaworthy."

Teddy motioned that there wasn't time to wait. "Okay, but isn't it funny?" She walked slowly down the steps.

"What's so funny?"

"Well, Mama always bakes bread and coffeecake on Thursdays and everything looks like she was ready to work but no Mama. Wonder if something happened."

"Oh, you're always imagining things. Papa probably was short of help in the store and Mama had to go in. You always worry too much. Come on, this is the most exciting day in our lives."

But Lisa insisted on making a quick search of the living room for her Brownie box camera so she could take photographs of the event. She was very proud of the camera even if it wasn't as fancy as those folding ones.

The living room and the dining room were separated by a curved arch, and all the walls in this area of the house were covered with heavy cream and white wallpaper with an embossed pattern of grapes. Lisa moved the pillows from one corner of the heavy stuffed chesterfield, but no camera. She straightened one of the starchy white doilies which had fallen from its position on a chair arm. She never understood why Mama placed ugly doilies all over the furniture.

Next, she removed a huge golden-haired Kewpie doll with a pink crocheted skirt from its place of glory on a rocking chair. Her camera wasn't there either. She pushed past the white wicker fernery with its many plants and noted the glass iced-tea set on the dining room table . . . so Mama hadn't planned on going out. Finally she spied the camera on the bottom level of the walnut tea wagon, resting on yet another embroidered organdy cloth.

The two of them quickly walked out the back door. Lisa glanced around the veranda, searching for Mike and Suzanne; but the golden oak glider swing was empty. Teddy gave it a push as they passed and the swing creaked forward as it hung suspended by two chains from the veranda ceiling. "Suzanne's probably skipping or playing jacks and balls, and I saw Mike with some boys blowing soap bubbles with his new pipe a while ago," he said.

The apple trees were almost ready for picking and the red cherries were already spoiling on the ground of the back garden. As they walked through their small orchard Lisa remarked again that this was the most beautiful town they had ever lived in. Papa had perpetually moved them all over Canada since she was a baby, but unquestionably this home in the Okanagan Valley of British Columbia was the most perfect. Secretly Lisa hoped that, having traveled all the way to this province on the Pacific coast, Papa finally planned to make this a permanent home.

The lake was just beyond a slight cliff at the bottom of their property and the two young people eagerly rushed down the sandy slopes toward the crowd of youngsters waiting for them. There, by the Katakala Lake, stood their pride and joy. The houseboat. Probably never before had there been anything like it on Katakala.

The boat was about eight feet long and only slightly curved at the prow and stern. The bottom was absolutely flat and the sides practically square. There were no portholes as they wanted no water seepage, and the cracks were filled with thick dark tar to make it seaworthy. On the deck, which was about five feet high, there was another boxlike projection, about four feet square. This they had named the bridge. Certainly every captain in the books they had read gave orders from a bridge. The sides of this bridge were marked with black stencils proclaiming REIKERS' CHEDDAR CHEESE THE FINEST IN B.C. A large tin tomato can, painted a bright red, sat on the very top. This was the sole smokestack.

"Perhaps if we gave the bridge another coat of white-wash we could erase those labels," Lisa remarked to her brother.

"My dad said we couldn't have no more paint to waste," answered a tow-headed boy standing beside her during the inspection.

"If we'd built the top ourselves the boat never would have been ready to sail this summer," another boy reminded them.

The ten children around the vessel all nodded their heads. They had had enough trouble collecting all the materials for the boat. Each could proudly point to some part of the boat that he had personally contributed. One had provided the lathes from his father's lumber yard; another had scrounged the tar, and a third had secretly borrowed nails from a keg at home.

It had taken them half the summer to build their ship. Teddy had originally inspired them to build it, but every one of them had played a major role. Inside the vessel was a narrow ladder leading down into the hold. In the future they planned to build bunks against the wall.

"It certainly looks great," Teddy said. They all nodded in agreement.

"It looks silly with those labels and how is anyone inside the bridgehouse going to look out or get any breath with that narrow window?" piped in a voice from the rear. Insulted, they turned to see Suzanne, Lisa's younger sister.

Ten-year-old Suzanne undoubtedly was the best looking of the four Stein children. She had very white skin without Lisa's bright freckles. Her hair, which hung in smooth ringlets, was a deep rusty red, and instead of wearing dirty overalls like her older brother and sister, she was clad in a pretty, flowered voile dress with a crocheted pinafore over it. Holding her hand was the youngest Stein, seven-year-old Mike. Their mother still called him her "baby" despite the fact that he weighed almost eighty pounds.

"Knew that I could smell a lemon from somewhere," mocked Teddy. "Miss Know-it-all Stein. You're never satisfied. Why didn't you do something if you're so smart?"

"You know that Papa forbade you to build this houseboat," Suzanne reminded him. "If I told Papa what you were doing when you were supposed to be delivering parcels to customers and weeding the garden, you'd get a licking. Papa warned you against spending time on *frivolous* things."

"But you also promised you wouldn't tell him, and you kept your promise," Lisa said. She smiled sweetly at her sister even though she took her threat seriously. Along with the brilliant auburn hair Suzanne had a tremendous temper and Lisa knew that, if pushed, Suzanne was capable of making trouble for all of them. "Maybe you'll help us make it look prettier, Suzanne. You're very artistic."

Feeling more important after this remark, Suzanne carefully inspected the boat. "I was just kidding. I'd never tell Papa. You know how he is."

Teddy touched the side of the boat where the words *Katakala Belle* were written. She really did look like some romantic Mississippi river boat. "Paint's dry now, let's go. And there's no wind on the lake. Perfectly calm for a launching. Come on."

The group had increased in size, for several spectators had joined them. As the crew focused their attention on Teddy's signal, four eager boys collided on the sand. As they pushed the vessel toward the water, one slipped on the wet sand and those behind toppled over him. Slowly they staggered forward, sinking in the sand. The harsh sound of the keel grinding in pebbles combined with the many human groans and grunts. They stopped momentarily while Teddy attached a heavy rope to a brass ring at the prow. "It'll drift away without it," he explained. Finally the stubborn boat neared the shoreline. Teddy and Jack climbed aboard while their friends continued to heave. The boat tilted to the right as the water finally spun around it. The working crew paused momentarily when they realized that the bank plunged down deeply at this spot.

"You get off there right away, Teddy Stein," Lisa shrieked.

"Will not, someone's got to be on the ship when she's launched. It's just a rip tide," he added pointing to the churning waters.

"Get off, Teddy, or I'll go find Mama," Lisa replied. "What if the boat isn't waterproof and you go down with her? We'd really be in trouble then. A fine skipper you'd be sitting at the bottom of the lake."

"Get me a life jacket, someone," Teddy commanded. There followed a frantic search in the rubbish pile near the shore, under a tarp and in the small tent that had been their headquarters during construction, but no life jacket was found.

"Darn you, Teddy, get off now. You can hold the rope. As a matter of fact you can have the honor of christening it," Lisa added, frightened now at the prospect of her daredevil brother going down with the untested vessel. What would Mama say? After all, Lisa was the oldest . . . and Papa; Papa would give it to them. Besides, Teddy really might drown. Lisa looked at the calm Katakala Lake and shivered. She sensed a growing wind and suddenly the lake looked dangerous. Perhaps the water spinning around farther from the shore was an undertow or perhaps even a whirlpool caused by the strong currents from the opposite shore.

Taking a deep breath, she made one final attempt to

stop him. "What if you get caught in the Whistling Whirlpool in the center there," she exclaimed, pointing toward the middle of the lake.

Teddy stopped immediately. All the others also turned toward her. Lisa felt her face turning a beet color. What a whopper this one was.

"Never did hear of the Whistling Whirlpool," Teddy replied, but his voice quivered as he looked toward the special spot. Several of their friends repeated the new name Lisa had invented and added variations. It all sounded scary and sort of delicious at the same time.

Teddy dropped off the deck, waded to shore, and grabbed the rope from Dick Richmond. He casually remarked that since he was the strongest, perhaps he had better hold the rope so the ship wouldn't be grounded. They all gave a final determined shove and the boat gurgled and groaned as it moved into deep water. Unmindful of the soaking their clothes received, the group gave the ship a last determined thrust and it glided away from the shore with the green waters lapping wildly around it.

They all stood silently admiring the masterpiece of two months' labor. The boat wobbled a bit, sank down a little, but otherwise appeared seaworthy. Teddy turned toward his sister and grinned. Little Mike jumped up and down and even Suzanne stopped playing the role of a proper young lady long enough to give a loud Indian war whoop.

"I'll just hand you the rope now, Dick, and I'll climb aboard," Teddy began, when abruptly a heavy hand settled on the back of his neck. "Owww, leggo, you idiot." Teddy wriggled to escape the powerful grip.

"Stop it, you hear, you foolish monkey. I'm not having

any son of mine drown. Nor any other child in this town," a harsh voice boomed.

Lisa turned around slowly to acknowledge that her worst fears had been fulfilled. "Papa," she whispered.

Out of the corner of her eye she watched Suzanne turn and slip unperceived up the hill toward home. Little Mike stood behind Lisa tugging at her arm. What a catastrophe! The group just stared at Papa. Embarrassed, she stood rigidly at attention like a soldier. Why did he always have to spoil their fun? It was bad enough that they had more chores than any other children in town, but on top of that he always seemed to ruin their plans. She turned to face her father, moving closer to Teddy who still clutched at the rope in a tight fist. All their friends had moved away as if they thought Papa would punish them too.

"Don't have to be a bunch of sheep," Papa muttered. "Just because Marilyn or Donny or Jerry has something doesn't mean you should also want it," he was forever saying.

Teddy mumbled that they had meant no harm, but Papa shook his head and clutched Teddy's collar as if he were an escaped convict. Lisa thought Papa looked ridiculous in his turned-up shirt-sleeves, business pants, thick red suspenders and gray spats over his shoes. He was such a small man, hardly taller than Teddy. With his round tummy and bald head he looked like one of those toy wooden roly polys that you were supposed to knock over with a ball. When he was really angry his accent became thick and his speech at the moment was almost impossible for an outsider to understand.

"Leggo that old rope you hear, kinder?" he shouted at Teddy. "Wondered where you were always wandering off to when I had things for you to do at the store. Want to get yourself all drowned, eh? Dummy. Mishegeneh. And you Lisa, taking your baby sister and brother down here. Thought you knew better. That's what they give you A's for in school, eh? For an empty head?"

Teddy let the rope slip out of his hand as Papa continued shouting. Lisa knew that Teddy also wished Papa would wait to bawl them out at home, not here before their friends. But when Papa became angry there wasn't much that anyone, even Mama, could do until he got rid of all that steam. As they stood obediently listening to him they heard a sudden hissing sound from the lake.

"Hey guys, look what's happening to the boat!" Dick shouted. Even Papa turned to the water. The rope had slipped into the lake and the boat had drifted toward the center while they had stood mesmerized by Mr. Stein. Pulled by a slight current, she had listed to the starboard, then floundered, and now water was pouring through all the carefully plugged cracks. The stricken vessel gave one final groan and then, with an agonized lurch, she sank below the surface of the lake. Within seconds only churning water remained to mark the spot where the boat had been floating.

They stood silently for a few minutes. At least Papa didn't make one of his remarks about how lucky they were to be alive. That would have been too much. "Oh no, no, it'll take months to build another one," Teddy whispered.

"You don't have to concern yourself about that, young man. You won't be building any more boats here. Where you're moving to there's no lake for your shenanigans," Papa retorted.

Both Teddy and Lisa turned and stared at him.

"We're going to move to another town, Papa? Won't go," Mike gulped as his tears began falling.

"You really don't want to stay in one place long enough for us to get settled in, do you, Papa? Always a spoilsport 'cause we've been here almost two years," Teddy added.

"How could you do it again, Papa? You promised," Lisa continued. Then, remembering their audience, she wheeled toward the hill and home.

Papa bit his underlip as if regretting his sharp words. Then gently he hoisted Mike to his shoulders. He beckoned Teddy to follow him and also began climbing.

An hour later, after they had changed to dry clothes, they sat stiffly in the parlor listening to Mama and Papa explain. Although Mama was taller than Papa, her slimness gave her a look of frailty. She kept patting Lisa on the head. Then she'd absently brush back her own graying hair into the tight neat bun at the back of her head.

"I didn't want your father to tell you suddenly like this," she was saying, "but I just found out myself an hour ago. Even left the bread to rise by itself. At this rate there won't even be a braided egg challah for Shabboth tomorrow evening." Her usually cheerful face was grim as she faced their father.

"Irving, Irving, I kept telling you. Not like this. I warned you they'd be disappointed. The children liked this town best. And who can blame them with the lovely lake and the mild weather?" Teddy and Lisa were still too stunned to respond. It was impossible to realize that they'd be leaving this wonderful place in a week. Forever.

Once again they were on the move and this time it would be good-bye to British Columbia. Papa had sold the store for a good price and had secretly purchased a large general store somewhere in Alberta, the neighboring province.

"Just imagine, children, all the way to the prairies of Alberta. Give you all an opportunity to see more of the world. Nothing like traveling. Wish that I had seen the world when I was young like you and didn't have to work. Just one little shtetl, town, in Europe until I was twenty years old . . . a filthy village in Russia with all us Jews jammed together in a small area . . . and I swore that when my chance came I'd keep moving until I saw the entire world. No one'd ever tell me I had to live on one wretched patch of land for the rest of my life."

Papa's forceful voice boomed out as he paced the room. Absently, he ran his thumbs under the braces which held up his pants. The elastics kept snapping to emphasize his feelings.

Teddy whispered under his breath to Lisa that it was fine for Papa, constantly moving, always buying a bigger store, meeting new people. Their father liked nothing better than meeting new people. But for them it became more difficult each time they transferred to another town. Lisa had been born in a place called Montreal, Quebec, which was on the St. Lawrence River in Eastern Canada; Winnipeg, which was in the central prairies, was listed on Teddy's birth certificate. Suzanne had been born in Vancouver, right on the Pacific coast, while Mike had come into the world while they were on a trip to Chicago, U.S.A. Neither Lisa nor Teddy remembered details concerning any of these places. They had been in so many towns since that time — not including the periods when Papa left them in some city while he traveled to the far north to sell supplies to remote settlements.

Mama didn't say much as Papa spoke. She never did. She sat there, in her dotted Swiss with lace on its organdy collar, and twisted the velvet ribbon on the neckline.

"I'll miss this house," she remarked quietly. "Nice living by the lake in a warm climate for a change. Reminds me a little of the other countries we were in before we came to Canada. It's a beautiful free land, but the winters are so long."

She gave a slight sigh, then noticed that her four children were close to tears. "You'll like it once you get there. Alberta's supposed to be a fine province. Lovely summers with not much rain. There's loads of snow for sledding in the winter and this time we'll only be forty miles from a big city."

"But Mama, we loved it here," Lisa cried. "We have to keep finding new friends all the time and this was such a perfect house."

"Edmonton's not far and we have relatives there. That'll be nice for a change," Mama continued.

"Oh, can we go into the city and get all dressed up and see an opera?" Suzanne asked. Suzanne always wanted to live in a big city so she could become an actress, and now she saw an opportunity to have her wish fulfilled.

"Even better than that, Suzanne," Mama replied. "You can take dancing lessons and Lisa will be able to play the piano again and Teddy can play the violin."

Teddy groaned. Lisa knew that he hated the violin. But she was excited to think she would finally learn how to play the old walnut piano. Mama had always promised her lessons but most of the towns they lived in didn't have music teachers or, if they did, the Steins moved away before Lisa had learned more than a few scales. She was beginning to think music teachers knew nothing but scales.

"Papa, can we build another boat there?" Mike asked.

"Well, I doubt if they have a lake there, sonny, but maybe a slough."

"If we go up to Edmonton, Papa, we could see the theater or some vaudeville. I'd really like to see some live actors perform. And since Edmonton's the capital of the province they should have real entertainment there," Teddy said.

"Just don't get any fancy-schmancy ideas about the stage, young man. It's bad business. Not for us. Remember my sister Ida? To you it could happen too."

"Oh, Papa, I just want to see some plays. You don't have to be so old-fashioned. Just because your sister Ida went off to Moscow to become an actress and married some Russian performer doesn't mean it's so terrible. This is Canada, and lots of my friends see plays without ruining their lives. It's not that village you always complain about."

"Aha, aha, so already he's an expert and making fun of his father. Give them an inch. . . . Listen to me, Mr. Know-it-all, my sister Ida was a tragedy, a waste. The theater stole her from our people, I tell you."

"Irving, enough already," Mama interrupted.

Teddy glared at his father, who shrugged his shoulders. "So maybe if you can keep your school marks high we might manage to see something," Papa said.

Lisa winked at Teddy and even managed a smile to Suzanne. Good report cards were important to their father. And perhaps Mama could persuade him this time. Papa was unquestionably the boss in the family, but he listened to their mother. Sometimes Lisa wished her father's rules were easier to understand. He was a concerned but strict parent. She wished that he was quiet and serene like the parents of her friends. He had a disastrous temper and, when angry, shouted at them in Yiddish. He talked of the wide world waiting for them, yet insisted on controlling every hour of their lives. Papa didn't know it, but they all loved the theater and acting. None of them had ever seen a really professional theater group but there had been occasional performers at the Elks Hall. Once they had seen a magician, but Teddy already knew the same tricks, and another time there had been an opera singer, but she'd been so fat and her voice so sour that they'd all covered their ears. So they preferred to read stories and poetry to each other and make up their own plays and charades.

"The town's not very big," Papa cautioned. "Under a thousand people, so don't expect a metropolis. But it's right smack in the middle of the finest wheat country in the world."

Lisa remembered something and dared to interrupt Papa. "Will we live in a house like this one, Papa?"

"Oh, I certainly hope so," Suzanne added. "With lots of bedrooms upstairs and not gloomy."

"Don't forget the veranda around the house. Even on a rainy day we can play there, Papa," Mike said.

"Oh, come on, you three. You really don't think he's going to find a home exactly like this one," Teddy said sarcastically.

Papa and Mama exchanged one of those funny glances adults reserve for each other, as if their children are half-wits or something. They switched to Yiddish, the Jewish language. Then the children were certain that something was wrong. Their parents always spoke English unless they had something very private to tell each other. They continued to speak rapidly and seemed to disagree about something.

Mama finally concluded the conversation. "Well, just let's say that our new home will be something completely different. Not like any homes we've lived in up until now. I won't say it is like this house, but . . . well, wait and you'll have a surprise."

"What's the name of the town, Papa? I'll go find it in the atlas."

"Chatko Falls."

"Strange name, Papa, must be an Indian name," said Teddy, as he pulled the atlas from a shelf. He looked carefully through the index and ran his finger across the map of Alberta, but found no Chatko Falls.

Papa shrugged and suggested that they start their packing. He lifted the trapdoor to the cellar and started dragging up the steamer trunk and the wardrobe trunks stored there. Lisa and Teddy showed each other crossed fingers as they pulled up the cases. "I just hope that Mama meant that the town will be a *happy* surprise," Lisa said.

2

A New World

THE DRIVE TO CHATKO FALLS seemed to take forever so that it was no wonder they were all fast asleep when they neared the district one hot summer morning.

Teddy had hoped that they'd travel by train so they might spend their nights in a pullman sleeper. They had taken the train once several years before. Suzanne still told Mike stories about the neat little green curtains that you closed around you at night when you were in your berth. It reminded Lisa of the picture in one of her books of Mistress Louisa, the princess who slept in a canopied bed with great side curtains.

"We have a new car and we will travel by car," Papa announced in a stubborn tone. "Besides, it will be a real education for you children to see the great country you live in."

Papa always gave lectures about the wonders of Canada.

"You can't believe how terrible life was in the old country. Half the people starved, and we lived in ramshackle wooden houses. And sometimes the Cossacks liked to set our homes on fire; just for fun, you understand."

"Tell us some more stories about when you were a boy, Papa," Mike would ask, as if he hadn't heard the stories a hundred times.

"Well, my papa died when I was only eight years old and my mother had so many children she had to send me into the city. And I became a weekly boarder at different homes. Had dinner somewhere else each night. How'd you like that, boychik? And mainly they gave me black bread and herring to eat, and when I went to school I always wore hand-me-down clothes that never fit." At that point he'd break off and tell them how important a good education was and they shouldn't take school for granted.

Lisa, half asleep as the car bumped over the waves of corduroy log road, had to admit that the most lovable thing about Papa was his gift for storytelling. He seemed to change character when he told them stories . . . even his harsh voice mellowed. Why, his stories were better than those of Scheherazade, and then she laughed out loud at the droll thought of comparing that fabled teller of the Arabian Nights with her portly father. When he was in a good mood he told stories for hours. Too bad that his good moods didn't last very long and were so far apart.

Their trip to Chatko Falls took more than a week. It had been very difficult to say good-bye to all their friends. Teddy whispered to Lisa that this was never again going to be a big problem. "Gee whiz, no sooner do you begin to feel at home with the gang than — 'Jack Robinson' — Papa has moved us again. We're the original nomads."

Lisa was afraid that Teddy might lose his temper with their father this time. Teddy kept saying that Papa was really a wandering gypsy. But instead of angry, Teddy seemed only bitter. He insisted that he wasn't going to bother making friends in the new town. He even left behind his precious rock collection, saying that in the future he'd stick to his books.

"I can pack up my books and take them with me no matter where we move, but there's no way you can pack up your friends and move them. That'd be nice, though . . . choose one of your friends from one of the dozen towns and then just take him down off the shelf, brush off the dust, and have someone to horse around with."

"Shush up, Teddy, with your grumbling. Papa's got to concentrate on the road," Mama warned from the front seat.

"I can't help it if Papa had to eat black bread and mush. What does he want us to do, eat it too?" Teddy responded. Papa stopped the car sharply and, with a single swift gesture, pivoted around in his seat and boxed Teddy's ear.

During the journey, Lisa didn't have any spare time to think about the past. She was far too involved in assisting Mama to keep the younger children quiet so that they didn't disturb Papa when he was driving. After all, it was a strenuous trip. The secondary roads they had to travel to get to Alberta were all rather dreadful, since there was no major highway connecting British Columbia to Alberta, even though they were adjoining provinces. Papa claimed that someday in the future there would be a great highway all across Canada, but in 1927 no such route existed. Mama laughed at Papa and said most people weren't as adventurous as their father and never would want to take such

long car trips. Besides, it would be very difficult to blast
a road through the Rocky Mountains.

As they wound their way down through the United
States and back up through southern Alberta, strangers
were always stopping Papa and asking questions about the
roads and routes he had taken. You'd think Papa was a
great explorer like Champlain, instead of a man who
merely had an itch when he stayed in any town very long.
People would drop by and look at their huge tent. They
also admired the new McLaughlin Buick touring car with
the bright yellow wheels and shiny black roof. Sometimes
it was great fun when Papa, who had a second sense regarding wonderful camping spots, stopped for the night
by a glistening lake or a huge forest.

Then there were other days when the flat tires or giant
potholes in some highways and narrow mountain roads
made the trip seem impossible.

On the narrow mountain roads they all got out and
shouted around the high curves, never daring to look
over the huge dropoff below them. "Stop, a car coming
through," they would caution. Most of the time the hair-
pin-curved roads were deserted, but on occasion there
would be another car hidden around the bend and then
Papa might have to back up a whole mile to let the other
car through the pass, since in some of these spots the
mountain roads were only wide enough for a single car.
Papa kept saying that if it was excitement the kids wanted,
then this trip offered far more than those silly radio programs or the silent movies.

Now they were on the final lap of their trip, and for the
past two days they had merely seen field after field of
golden wheat, with the skyline broken every so often by

the bright beacons of the red grain elevators. While Papa talked of the rich western soil and the perfect climate, Mama reminded him that it must be very cold in winter with those flat fields offering so little protection from the winds. Mama still remembered the year they had lived in Manitoba.

They sighted the huge black water tower of a large town and they assumed they were at their destination. Little Mike kept calling it a "water bottle" and wanted to climb it. "Sorry, nope, that's not Chatko, but this is one of the nearest major towns," Papa volunteered. "Here's where we switch to a dirt road and follow it for six miles until we see a deep ravine with a deserted mill. Then turn off for Chatko."

"You mean there isn't even a road marker for directions?" Lisa asked.

No one seemed prepared to answer her question except Teddy, who clowned beside her. He put his hand above his eyes as if searching in the distance. "Hallooooooo there, has anyone seen a little town? We lost it someplace. Look at your compass, traveler, then bear to the southeast. I hear the place is somewhere out there."

Suddenly they passed the mill and Papa had the car in second gear as they chugged down a steep clay gully. Ahead lay a flat valley. Suzanne and Mike awoke from their naps and, pulling up the side blinds on the windows, pushed their heads out to see their new town.

"Papa, this can't be it. There's only about ten big buildings and one, two, four, five blocks of houses," Suzanne whined as she counted.

"There isn't any water bottle. I want a water bottle," wailed Mike. "All towns have water bottles."

"The only running water in Chatko is in the streams or sloughs," Papa said.

"Omigosh but it's ugly," said Lisa staring at the town. "It's a disaster."

"It's nowhere," Teddy cracked, voicing their mutual sense of betrayal.

Mama bit her lip as she cuddled Mike closer to her chest. "No jokes, Irving. You're just stopping here for gas?"

Surely this remote little village, where there was only a single spur-line railroad track with no station, was not their destination. Papa turned crimson to the top of his shiny pate and his knuckles, gripping the steering wheel, were like a line of chalky marbles. He refused to speak, but soon a peeling sign which hung at an angle from a bent post confirmed their fears.

"Well maybe it's not the Garden of Eden, but —"

"Actually it's a paradise — for fools," Teddy retorted.

It was a hamlet, not a town. Surrounded by a grove of tall trees, it lay there silent and exhausted like a tired old tramp, with fields stretching away as far as they could see. If you squinted your eyes, Lisa thought, the fields appeared to melt into a blue, flat ocean which was really the sky. Even the quiet main street was a mass of holes with a warning sign stuck in front of one pothole that appeared huge enough to swallow the entire car. At that moment Lisa wished that Papa would drive straight into the hole. In addition to the four formal blocks of houses, there were many clusters of dwellings which just seemed to have sprouted from thickets of trees, and these unplanned sites gradually disappeared into the fields and trees on the edge of the town. All the narrow, square wooden houses were weatherbeaten and peeling as if the occupants had finally given up trying to fight the seasons. With their graying exteriors and many rickety side sheds, they were hardly a warming sight. There were no trees on the village streets, almost as if someone had a grudge against nature and had chopped them down out of spite.

As they drove down the main street they picked out the barber shop, poolhall, post office, two churches at either end of the block, blacksmith and feed store, a grocery, a community hall, bank and butcher shop. Smack at the end of the block stood the general store.

Undoubtedly it was the most striking building in the town. It stood two stories high and seemed to consist of two buildings of completely different vintage and architecture which had been accidentally united. One building was flat-roofed and square and appeared to be made of rough wood. The other was a broad two-story affair with gabled windows and a shingled roof. But it was the incredible color of the building which gave it such an unusual air. It was painted the most violent, shiny purple shade imaginable.

"Oh my God, what have they done, I said dark brown, not purple," Papa said. He stopped the car abruptly by two leaning gas pumps in front of the store and motioned for all of them to climb out. Lisa noticed that there was also a hitching post beside the pumps.

"Can't we see our house first before we go into the store?" Teddy asked. Teddy could always be counted upon to recover from any surprise.

"This is our home," Mama said, motioning upward to the second floor of the frame building.

"My gosh, we've lived in a lot of strange places before, but never above a store," Lisa whispered to Teddy.

"What will all the kids think of us, living in such a hideous place . . . what a color," Suzanne mumbled.

"Just think how you'll never have to run downtown if you want Mama or something. She'll be right below you," Papa said.

"And so will the store full of people," Teddy muttered.

Even Papa appeared to realize that there was something unique about this building. He defended it more strongly than he had any previous place. He explained that there were two staircases to the house. One was inside the store and the other, an outdoor staircase, was around the back of the building. The pump, from which they'd get their daily water supply, was at the rear along with an outhouse.

Lisa didn't dare look at Mama as they walked up to the big purple door at the front of the store. She knew that it would hurt Mama even more if she saw the tears begin to fall down Lisa's cheek. Mama always counted on Lisa. She called her "my sensible child." But today Lisa didn't feel at all practical. Her tummy felt all woozy, like the time she and Teddy had devoured an over-ripe watermelon. Her fingers, twisting the gold locket around her neck, were moist and sticky. What had Papa gotten them into this time?

At least in the past there had always been a house with a big backyard. But this miserable purple store just stood like a stupid monster in the middle of nowhere. There were no trees to climb or hang a rubber tire from. Just a dusty road and an old wooden sidewalk that seemed to curve up and down like a roller coaster at an amusement park.

"You the crazy folks goin' to live in the Purple Folly?"

a thin voice asked. They turned to see a scrawny urchin, who could have been of either sex, staring at them. "My pap said you must have rocks in your heads to paint a buildin' this color." Papa glared at the child, who backed away and raced down the block.

Papa turned a giant key on a wooden paddle in the keyhole of the door and urged them to enter. "It really is great inside," he mumbled sheepishly. "Has a gigantic candy display. You kids will be in charge of running the candy counter."

3

Exploring the
"Purple Folly"

Lisa had to admit that the store was much more enticing inside than out. It was the largest general store that she had ever seen, other than the department stores in big cities. It seemed to extend back in the gloom as far as she could see. The front sections were bright and well-lighted from the large windows but the back portion was dim, depending on the whims of irregularly placed ceiling lights. The oiled wooden floors were cool after the heat outside, so they all moved quickly to explore the interior.

The first building housed the grocery and dry goods center. There were two massive wooden counters extending almost the entire length of the building. To their left was an attractive glassed-in candy display. It stood right behind four huge blocks of salt, two blocks rust-colored and two white. Mike put his tongue against a white block

only to have his mother jerk him away. "You're not a cow, are you, Mike? Those are for cows to lick, not people."

The candy cupboards were divided into about twenty small sections and were filled to the top with everything from jawbreakers to cinnamon sticks and Turkish delight.

"Oh, Teddy, look at the adorable little shovels for measuring the candy with," Lisa said. But Teddy was sniffing at the various barrels clustered around the counter.

He pulled bars of lemon soap from one, peanuts from another, a wet molasses finger emerged after he checked a third, and finally a handful of crackers from yet another. There were also huge sacks of sugar, flour and rice piled up neatly in front of the counter.

Receiving permission from her father, Suzanne carefully lifted the heavy glass lid off a round of cheddar cheese resting on a wooden platter. "Come on, let's have a picnic, we'll surely never go hungry here." Then they all dug into the huge cheese round.

Lisa decided that Chatko Falls might not be too bad after all. This was the most intriguing store she had ever seen.

"Just think, children, you're all going to help us manage the store. It's so spread out that I'll need all of you to help serve people. You see, our busiest time will probably be Saturday afternoon and night when the farmers can get in." Pleased that they too were to be the proprietors of this impressive place, they began exploring.

The dry goods section was at the rear of groceries. Here they found dozens of bolts of cloth, cardboard packets of buttons, needles, and patterns. Suzanne draped a remnant of bright silk around her shoulders and popped a straw hat with red cherries on her head. "Hey, this is almost better

than a five-and-ten-cent store in the city. Just think what
fun we can have when we play dress-up. May I serve you,
madame?" She curtseyed to an invisible customer.

Papa urged them to walk under the arch which divided
the two halves of the store. While there was no partition
between the two buildings, each had a separate entrance
for customers. The mating of the wooden building with
the older log structure was like attaching the rear of a
dachshund sausage dog to the front of a German shepherd.
Ludicrous.

This building housed the hardware and kitchen items.
The back section was men's wear with the counters piled
high with work pants, overalls, double fleece-lined underwear, work shirts and rubber and felt boots. Under the
counter were shoeboxes with a rusted ice cream parlor
metal chair and matching footstool for assisting customers.
Permeating the area was the smoky smell of buckskin
gloves and mitts. Dangling from the rear ceiling by wire
were rods displaying ties and socks. Several cylindrical
cardboard hatboxes stood against the wall with an assort-
ment of straw hats piled precariously on top of them. Papa
drew in his breath and blew a mass of dust off the hats.

In the front portion horse halters, kerosene lanterns and
oil cans hung from pegs in an overhead beam. Kegs of nails
jostled for position with enamel basins, chamber pots,
barrel churns and tire pumps.

Reaching over a pile of inner tubes, Papa pointed to an
open crate which stood taller than Mike. It was a strange
awkward machine unfamiliar to any of them. The thick,
footed metal base had two circular round platforms stick-
ing out, what looked like a milk can with spigots, a crank,
and a huge metal bowl on top.

"Is it a new-fangled soda fountain, Papa?" Mike inquired.

"Just brought in this new King Cream Separator. It's good for up to fifty cows, real big capacity," Papa replied.

Mike politely asked what the cows did with the machine.

"Why it skims off cream from the milk, faster than you'd believe," Papa laughed. "You kids better start learning about life in the country. There won't be any milk wagon with horses coming to our door now. Get it right fresh from the farm. No iceman, either."

"You can't be serious, Papa."

"You'll get used to it. Most of the families in this district haven't any electricity, so don't think you're hard done by without indoor plumbing. Our life is mighty easy compared with our neighbors."

While they absorbed this new way of living they moved toward a glass-front showcase. Kegs of nails and coils of wire and hemp blocked their view, but Papa reached under the showcase and pulled out some navy velvet boxes. "Here's a special gift for each of you, imported harmonicas." And he handed lovely silver mouth organs to each of them. Even Mama was smiling now.

Lisa crinkled her freckled nose as she absorbed the clean smell of kerosene. Then it finally occurred to her to ask about the upstairs apartment. "After all, Papa, that's where we'll be living."

"Had it all cleaned up 'specially for you, and the furniture will arrive here by truck within the next couple of days." Then Papa led them to the rear warehouse of the building. It was dark there with only a few bare light bulbs dangling from long cords. "Only general store in the area with total electricity," he proudly told them.

Lisa was grateful that some of the buildings had electric light. Now she wouldn't have to clean smoky lamp chimneys. If only there had been indoor plumbing — but that was expecting too much.

"Oh, Lisa, Lisa, come quick. The staircase is hidden like a secret passage in this warehouse back here," Teddy called. Sure enough, there, behind giant crates of eggs, was a closed door sheltering the stairway.

Lisa dashed up the narrow steps behind Teddy. "If only there is a room just for me alone, Teddy, a tiny room, that's all I need. Mike doesn't bother you at night, but I hate always having to share with Suzanne. She's so inquisitive I have no privacy."

"Don't step on any cracks then." Teddy grinned down at her. "Maybe if you don't you'll have some luck and get your wish."

She slowed her upward pace, cautiously tiptoeing around the dangerous chinks in the stairs as they had done when they were very young. When they arrived puffing at the top, Papa led the way down a narrow storage corridor to the apartment.

Mama looked at the giant black nickel-trimmed stove that dominated the kitchen. She gingerly found a stove lifter and peered into the six holes on top. "Looks clean for a change, but it will sure eat up a lot of coal and wood. And someone will have to carry all that wood and coal up the stairs every day." She added, "And fill the cistern with water."

Teddy wrinkled his nose considering the woodpile, his future chore. Lisa thought longingly of a gas stove which meant no ashes to clean out, nor any messy polishing.

On the other hand, what could be cozier on a chilly

morning than the chance to open the oven door of a wood stove and bask in its warmth as she put on her clothing?

Lisa skipped quickly through the dining room, then past the living room and started counting bedrooms. The large one facing the main street belonged to Papa and Mama, the one next to it was for Suzanne, and a big back one for the boys, but where was a private place for her?

"There are only three bedrooms," she said accusingly.

"What did you expect, a palace with seven?" Papa retorted. "I think we have a very large place here, for a store."

Mama, who had been opening all the cupboards to check storage areas, turned to her with sympathetic eyes. "Poor Liseleh, someday there will be a home with a little room for you alone — but you'll just have to wait."

"Unless she wants to sleep in this giant pantry," Teddy called from behind them. "Look here, we could each have a shelf to sleep on just like on our ship and there'd still be room for groceries."

Lisa ran to the cupboard which muffled Teddy's voice. It was the most massive pantry she had ever seen. It even had a tiny opening high up in the wall. Afraid to appear foolish, she stood there silently chewing on the elastic of her braid. Finally she could contain her idea no longer.

"Oh please, Mama, please, Mama. Just look at this. There are plenty of other closets in the house. Teddy could help me knock out the shelves and not take up any of Papa's time. There's just enough space for a small bed over here. And Mama, I'd be a bigger help than ever if I had a place that was all my own with some privacy. Suzanne always takes up the whole bed at night and she wakes me up talking in her sleep. Oh please, Mama dear."

"Just need a small pane of glass in that space up there and Lisa'd have enough sun to keep her healthy all year," Teddy said. He showed Mama the window, blocked by two nailed boards. "Come on, Mama, give Lisa a break. If she's willing to stay in this cubbyhole herself, why not let her?"

"But the other room is plenty big enough for both of them," Papa said, peering through the door.

"We could have a hired girl to share the room with Suzanne this way," Lisa said. " 'Specially if you're going to work all the time in the store, Mama, and it looks like Papa will need you since the store is so big." Mama was always interested in practical matters. Perhaps this suggestion might sway her. Her mother put her hands together over her lips and glanced at Papa.

"Well, I suppose you're getting to be a young lady now and could use some privacy. And it might be a good idea to get some help in here. Not much room for a dresser, though, and where in the world would you study?" Mama said.

Lisa knew that she was finally going to have her private room because when Mama ordinarily said no, she never left the conversation open for any "ifs" or "buts." "Teddy and I always study together, don't we, Ted?" He nodded.

A few hours later Lisa helped Mama serve their first dinner on sawhorses and planks. "Children, have some more to eat," Mama insisted. She was always pushing more food at them. Mama appeared to believe that everyone had huge stomachs. Lisa wondered if Mama would finally stop demanding that they clean their plates if they became as heavy as the fat woman in the traveling circus. It was impossible to swallow food today; there were so many new experiences to think about.

Lisa was no longer disturbed about their new home. Their own furniture would be in place the following day. And so what if all the children in the town made jokes about the Purple . . . what did they call it? Oh yes, The Purple Folly. Now she finally had her very own room. Papa had promised that he'd have a handyman pull down the shelves. And he even gave her permission to choose whatever color of paint she wanted from the store below. She already knew she'd paint the room pink. There was a can in the store labeled sunrise pink; it would be lovely, particularly after the bleak tan walls in all the other bedrooms she had ever slept in. Perhaps Mama might let her use some paint to cover up the dark walnut surface of her dresser. And she'd make a stool from one of those empty kegs in the hardware section and find some material to cover it with. And she'd finally hang all the pictures she'd clipped from old magazines. Mama had never allowed this before because the thumbtacks left marks on the wall, but in a cupboard, who'd care? Then she'd be able to go to sleep staring at beautiful things instead of those gloomy paintings of chubby people in funny old-fashioned clothes that Mama had all over the place.

Suzanne walked to the living room window which viewed the entire little town. A small group of children clustered across the street from the store, pointing up at her window. "I just bet they're making fun of us in our new home," she said to Lisa, who was clearing the table.

"Sure, bet they're asking a lot of nosy questions about us," Mike replied.

"And the first few days they'll be whispering about us,"
Teddy said.

School started Monday. It always gave Lisa a funny feeling in the pit of her stomach that first day at a new school,
although she wasn't going to share this thought with
Suzanne. But it wasn't really going to be too bad, when
she finally had her own private room. And after all, how
many kids had a chance to live above a store anyway?

4

Lisa Faces a Crisis

AUTUMN WAS LISA'S FAVORITE season of the year. Perhaps it was because her birthday fell in October, or maybe it was the marvelous colors the trees and bushes wore at this time of the year. The deep crimsons, burnt oranges and glowing yellows always made this season seem like a costume ball for the poplars and birches of the countryside. Lisa especially loved the sound of her firm footsteps as they crunched over dry, fallen leaves. However, this first fall in Chatko Falls was just plain depressing, despite the festive hues of the landscape.

As she assisted Lucy, their hired girl, in sweeping the back steps, she made a wry face, remembering the devastating first day of school the previous month.

What ignoramuses they had been as they headed for school!

"But Papa," Teddy had later reported, "it wasn't just

a small school. It had *only* four rooms with sixty students for all eight grades."

"Irving, at least you should have checked the school before buying the store," Mama had replied in a stern tone, "and Lisa tells me there were only four other children in the eighth grade. Why, she'll have to take a bus or something to get to high school in another town next year. The school doesn't even go past the eighth grade."

Teddy and Lisa were stunned to hear Mama addressing Papa in this manner. She was always most polite in speaking to him. Yet it had been shattering to find that this was merely a four-room schoolhouse. Even more disturbing was the behavior of the other children in the school. When the four Steins had first entered the building with their books and pencil boxes clutched tightly in their hands along with their old report cards, everyone had immediately started giggling. "Why, the Purple Folly people are here."

"Look at those fancy-pantsy clothes, eh."

"Hey, dandies, city slickers, don't get manure on your boots," Rolf Ogden, the local bully, had snorted.

After the teacher had assigned her a seat, Lisa studied her fellow students. Only then did she realize that her family was hopelessly overdressed for this small rural school. Mama had insisted they wear better clothing for the first day of school, but what a mistake! Coming from a large town in a different province, how were they to know that these sturdy country children wore nothing but the most durable of garments?

After all, the majority of the local students came directly from their farm homes, after completing early morning chores. Some walked several miles to school; others arrived in the family wagon, and still others were fortunate enough to come on their own horses. What a shock to see those animals tied to a high fence adjoining the school grounds!

Lisa cringed, remembering how ignorant she had been. She had spent hours with Mama searching for her new middy blouse and navy serge skirt before they left B.C.

The blouse was most attractive with its broad sailor collar trimmed with gold braid. The left sleeve bore an embroidered anchor while the wide hip-height belt fastened with brass buttons. And the tie matched the navy blue of the skirt. She had tied back her straight black hair with a huge red bow instead of keeping it in the usual pigtails.

All the girls back home had worn huge bows on top of their heads. That first morning not one girl in the room had a ribbon in her hair. Here they used elastics and bobby pins. Instead of hip-length blouses the girls wore flowered cotton dresses or unfitted homespun-weave shifts of muddy, somber colors.

And how they stared at Teddy with his tweed golf cap and knickerbocker breeches which ended just below the knee. It was certainly fortunate that Mama hadn't been able to persuade him to wear his belted corduroy jacket. All the boys wore heavy denim work pants or bibbed overalls over their flannel shirts. Overalls in school had been strictly forbidden in their former community.

Teddy glared back at Rolf, whose blond hair hung in a semi-circle around his head as if someone had inverted a bowl on top of his hair and then just cut roughly around it. However, while Rolf looked peculiar to them, several other boys sported the same bizarre style.

At recess, Suzanne had tossed her curls disdainfully and

said that she didn't care one little bit. She would not change. Much to Lisa's surprise, before the month was over, most of the girls in Suzanne's class had their fair hair covered with tortured dangling ringlets in imitation of Suzanne's natural curls. Suzanne's only complaint was that the teacher forbade her to use her new self-filling fountain pen. Instead, she insisted they bring a pen holder and metal nibs to improve their penmanship. Suzanne resented using the delicate nib pen which often splattered blue ink over her clothing, and she detested the ugly blotches of running ink it left on the pages.

Several of the girls were curious about the store and Lisa invited them over, generously handing out big bags of candy. But Papa refused to allow that to go on for long.

"You don't want to bribe them into being your friends, do you, Lisa?" Teddy said. "And who wants that kind of friends anyway?"

Two months dragged by. Here it was late October, a Saturday morning at that. There was no Saturday afternoon movie matinee in Chatko either, and the only person Lisa could talk to was Lucy. Lucy was nice, but being four years older than Lisa, she was more interested in discussing her boyfriends than anything else.

Their parents had gone to Edmonton early in the morning to buy supplies for the store and to visit relatives. Before their departure Lisa had promised to help supervise activities in the store and to watch the kids. Oh, if only Mama and Papa had taken her along with them. She wanted an opportunity to meet her Edmonton cousins and longed to ride on a streetcar again.

But Lisa was happy that Teddy had finally found a

friend. Late in the afternoon he had brought a quiet boy, his own age, upstairs and announced that they were going down the road to explore some streams.

"It's awfully chilly today, Teddy, might even snow. Why don't you wait until Mama's back tomorrow? You can sense the weather change in that sharp wind and look how dishwater gray the sky is."

"Come on, Sis, cut your descriptions. Jacky says he knows this stream real well, and we'll be home by suppertime. Just 'cause you have to stay cooped up here doesn't mean we all need to suffer."

With Teddy gone, Lisa found it difficult to concentrate all afternoon. Not satisfied with staring constantly for a sign of him through the window, she kept going to the door and peering down the street. Customers entering the store in the late afternoon blew on their hands to get warm and said they could smell snow in the air.

"Temperature must of dropped fifteen degrees in the past hour or so," one man complained as she handed him his change.

When Lisa locked the store at six o'clock Teddy still hadn't appeared. "Lucy, it's late and that wind is whistling through the doors. Any idea what stream they could have gone to?"

Lucy, carrying plates to the table, shook her head. "Only stream I know around here is too swift for them to go in. Near Wilders' farm."

"Where's Wilders' farm? Think I could find it myself? Teddy's never late like this."

"Nah, you'd never find it, 'specially now that it's getting dark. It's down a ravine up the road a ways."

"Well, there must be somebody who'd help me," Lisa replied as Suzanne returned from her window watch to shake her head negatively.

"I'll go with you, Lisa, but it's sort of spooky out there the way that wind's blowin'," Mike said.

"Well, you might go get Macnamara, he's sort of the patrolman hereabouts. Real good-looking too. But have your dinner first."

Lisa didn't wait for dinner but dashed, with her open coat flying, down the outdoor stairs to find Macnamara.

When she finally found him, Macnamara told her not to worry — although a frown creased his forehead. He wanted to walk her back to the store before beginning a search but she insisted on accompanying him. As they passed the store she saw her younger sister and brother still peering out of the upstairs window. She trudged behind the shaky beam of the flashlight the patrolman carried.

"I never should have let him go. I just knew I was wrong. How long will it take to get there?"

"Maybe we'll stop and get a couple of fellows to help us in case they're lost. Not that it's too likely." He shone his flashlight into the prairie ahead of them. Now luminous snowflakes made it impossible to see clearly across the flat plain.

"Hey there, that you, kids? Isn't that your brother down there a ways?" Macnamara started to run in the direction of the small bedraggled figure stumbling toward them.

"What's wrong with him? He looks wet or something," Lisa replied as she rushed toward the figure momentarily outlined by the beam of light. "Teddy, what happened? Where have you been?" she called.

Macnamara didn't waste any time on words as he dashed toward Teddy. "Darn fool kid, bet you fell in that stream, that's what you did. Picked a miserable night for it too." Teddy just stood quivering with a tattered blanket around his shoulders.

"Like a wet rat," Macnamara continued, as they hustled Teddy toward the store. "Get him out of those duds fast, girl.

"I'll just pop in a moment with you and tell Lucy to get a hot bath for him. By gosh, he'll get one devil of a cold from that soaking, he sure will."

While Lucy and Macnamara dragged the huge corrugated tub into the kitchen, Lisa started several pots of water heating on the stove. "Get right out of those clothes, Teddy Stein, you're shaking something awful.

"Lucy, could you stop talking to Mr. Macnamara long enough to get some more pails of water?" Lucy blushed but Macnamara was delighted to help her pump water for the tub.

"It was the best fun yet, Lisa," Teddy confided when he was finally wrapped up in a huge eiderdown. "But the stream ran so fast and when I bent to pick up this nice hunk of wood floating by, why I just got pulled in with it. And the walk home! Jacky found me a horse blanket someplace but it was so cold and dark."

"Never mind what fun it was. Get right in this tub now before you get sick," she had replied.

It was about four A.M. when she awoke to see little Mike standing at the bottom of her bed. Mike was still rubbing the sleep out of his eyes. "He woke me up Lisa, woke me up. Not my fault. He won't stop making terrible noises, like a wolf. Thought the wolves had gotten in my room and I went to tell Teddy; he was the one making the funny sounds. I think something's wrong with him, Lisa."

Lisa didn't wait to hear any more but jumped out of bed and rushed toward the boys' room with Mike trailing behind her. Teddy was sitting up in his bed with his hand over his chest. "My chest, it aches, Lisa, and when I cough it's like I'm caught in the wringer of the washing machine. It hurts to breathe." Teddy clutched the eiderdown closely around him and bit his bottom lip. Lisa motioned Mike to go and awaken Lucy and bent to feel Teddy's forehead.

By the time Lucy arrived with Mike, Lisa had already taken Teddy's temperature with the thermometer from Mama's medicine chest. Surely Lucy would know what to do next. She whispered to Lucy that the thermometer had registered a hundred and five degrees.

"He's like fire, he's so hot, Lucy. What shall we do now?"

"Gee, I don't know, Lisa. Maybe I should go out and pump some cold water and my mom always said herb tea cured anything. Maybe you should make some, but — but I don't remember the recipe. Mom always took care of everyone when they were sick."

"Lucy, go get the doctor, then." Lisa knew that whatever it was, Teddy was extremely ill, and Lucy obviously was not going to be of any great assistance. The doctor was the answer, and then they could put cold compresses on Teddy's head like Mama did. She had no idea what Mama put in the compresses but that had always been the cure — and some hot lemonade. Somewhere there must also exist the ingredients for a mustard plaster to put on his chest.

"There ain't no doctor in Chatko Falls, Lisa."

Lisa stared at her in total shock. "But there has to be someone. His fever is dangerous, and he can't stay like this. What about a druggist?"

"Nearest doctor is in Edmonton or in Whistling Creek and you ought to know we don't have a drugstore."

Sending Lucy to pump some cold water, Lisa quickly applied compresses to Teddy's head. She then forced two aspirins down his throat and bundled flannel across his chest with Lucy's assistance, for Teddy was now totally limp. She then told Suzanne, who stood anxiously by the bed with Mike, to find Miss Wells, the telephone operator, and get her to open the telephone exchange so that she could phone her parents in Edmonton.

"But Miss Wells is sleeping by now," Lucy insisted.

"The two of you go and wake her up even if you have to pound and shout for an hour or break a window with a rock. It's an emergency. Tell her. And then see if you can find Mr. Macnamara again; he must know someone in town who can help us." Both girls rushed out the door, relieved to be given some direction.

Lisa forced another aspirin down Teddy's throat and changed the cool compress. She stared at all the bottles in her mother's kit but it was useless. What good was iodine, castor oil and Epsom salts? Teddy was so feverish now that he forcefully threw the covers on the floor. Then a few moments later he shivered at the bottom of the bed, begging for a hot water bottle. His breath was labored, and a dull rattling sound came when he coughed.

Four hours later she sat dozing by the bed. She had finally reached Mama on the phone and her parents said they would soon be there with a doctor. She had sponged Teddy with the alcohol and water combination Mama had told her about on the phone. Although she had repeated this process many times his fever always went up again. When she awoke from her brief nap to see Mike changing the compresses again, she didn't even bother to brush away the tears that slid down her face. Her most beloved brother was dying. She was certain. He lay very silent and quiet with the perspiration highlighting the dark tan face. If only she were a nurse like Florence Nightingale. Macnamara had brought over two of the neighborhood ladies early in the morning but they hadn't been of much help.

"Macnamara came to get me while I was taking in my laundry early this morning; said how deathly sick your brother took. Pity your ma went and left you all alone. Brought a jar of honey and some herbs my sister-in-law swears by," said Mrs. Suderman, pushing past Lisa to the bedroom.

"I'm Mrs. Hansen and when I saw them gallivanting down the road thought maybe somebody died," said the heavy lady beside her. Mrs. Hansen still had on a faded flannel kimono and her head was covered by a profusion of white rags she had worn overnight to make her hair curly.

"My, don't he look just like the frozen sheets I took off the clothesline a minute ago. All white and stiff just like 'em," said Mrs. Suderman. "Boil them herbs for an hour. Smell bad, but nothing like them for a poultice. Draws out infection."

Lisa took the paper bag but the ladies offered no new advice. The tall, gaunt Mrs. Suderman just kept clucking right over Teddy's head.

"No hope there," said Mrs. Hansen. "He's going to burn up with that fever."

"He will not die. Lisa won't let him die," Mike had answered, shaking his fist at the women. "How would you feel if someone talked like that in front of you . . ." And then Mike too had been silent as he turned to watch Teddy lying there as still as the ladies had predicted.

It was almost noon, and Lisa and Lucy had sponged Teddy a dozen times more, when Papa and Mama arrived with the doctor. They gently led Lisa out of the room as the doctor examined Teddy.

"Come on, Lisa, it wasn't your fault," Suzanne said as they all waited on the big horsehair sofa in the parlor. "No way you could prevent Teddy from falling in the stream."

"He'd never have gotten a chill if I'd made him stay here."

"Golly, Lisa, nobody'd ever believe that snow comes so quick to a place," Mike added.

"Lisa, look; I want you to take my turquoise ring that Papa brought me from Montreal. It's my favorite belonging and it's special from me to you."

Lisa tried to refuse the delicate ring Suzanne pressed upon her. She shook her head silently and waited for the doctor to finish his examination of Teddy.

Their mother came out once or twice and Papa put his arms around her. None of the children had ever seen their parents embracing like this. It seemed a very bad sign to all three of them. Papa had tears in his eyes, and they all knew that their father absolutely never cried. Macnamara entered their home briefly to receive a prescription from Papa to be filled at the drugstore in Whistling Creek. It seemed only minutes later that they heard the car return. Macnamara had driven so fast that puffs of dust remained on the street long after he had dashed back up the steps.

Lisa didn't know how long she had slept but a soft touch on her arm brought her back from a dream where she had been chasing across a field after Teddy and she called his name. The strange doctor, with his thin gray hair falling untidily across his face, was whispering to her. "You're a very brave and sensible girl, Lisa. Good head on your shoulders."

"But it was all my fault. I shouldn't have let him go." She didn't dare ask him if Teddy would live. As long as she held back the fatal question he might be fine. "What is it?" she mumbled.

"Pneumonia, and there might be some other complications."

"We must take him to a hospital then," Papa said. Mama was weeping.

"The hospital is too far away to risk it. He still has a high fever and shortness of breath. I hope that with the medicine we now have the worst will soon be over. There are no miracle drugs for pneumonia, Mrs. Stein . . . perhaps someday. Your daughter here did everything I myself would have prescribed. Good head, young lady." The kindly man absently patted her shoulder again.

Now she really couldn't hold back her tears any longer. Pneumonia was such a frightening word. Lisa threw her arms around Mama and buried her head in the familiar chest. Mama was still wearing her good city clothes and Lisa felt her lapel watch scratch her cheek.

Mama held her tightly and murmured something about her good girl. Suzanne and Mike burst through the door and also snuggled up to Mama. Their father sat down in a chair and stared through the picture hanging before him.

"This is a horrible nasty town and if we had stayed in our real home Teddy'd be fine now," Suzanne shouted. "It's this wretched place that did it." Mama roughly clamped her hand over her younger daughter's mouth but it was too late and the room became silent.

Suddenly Lisa remembered the old nursery rhyme: "If wishes were horses, beggars would ride/If turnips were watches, I'd wear one at my side." Just wishing would not make Teddy better, and he was certainly not the first person to take sick in a town without doctors.

Papa remained sitting like a stone and Mama was too busy with the younger children to notice. Belatedly Lisa realized that Papa might have been hurt by Suzanne's unthinking remark. Lisa always had been rather timid with her father, but somehow she knew she must now cross the wide room and do something to prevent him from blaming himself. Maybe it was some inner instinct, like that of a migratory bird, which forced him to move constantly from town to town. After all, birds had to go south in winter no matter what.

She disentangled herself from the octopus of arms around Mama and hesitantly moved across the room. When she stood before her father she regretted her gesture. He hadn't noticed her. He slumped in his chair. "Papa, Teddy asked for you last night," she stammered.

"He really did?" She nodded her head. But then another thought occurred to him. "And I wasn't there to help him."

Had she made things worse by her remark? She could almost taste the bitterness in his voice. Quickly she continued. "And he said what a wonderful fishing spot he's found down by that stream and he'd like to tell you about it."

Papa almost smiled then and rose from the chair. "Hear that, Esther? He asked for me. There's something special about Teddy." Then, as if responding to some preset signal, both parents left the room, Mama to arrange dinner and Papa to check with his clerk.

Two hours later the doctor came from Teddy's room. "By Jove, he's a tough boy. He's going to make it. The fever is dropping and his breathing is much better. Got a lot of courage, that boy of yours. Complains of pain in his joints but he has fewer chest pains now."

When the doctor finally departed he suggested that Lisa be allowed to see Teddy for a few moments. The room was in semi-darkness with just a single light glowing from a corner lamp. Lisa leaned over a shadowy Teddy. He appeared to be asleep; while his face was waxy and drawn, no longer did his lips show a bluish discoloration. His silence made it difficult to accept the doctor's positive diagnosis. Forgetting her promise, she leaned over, hoping to hear his heart beat. As she straightened up, his eyelids blinked open as rapidly as those of a china doll.

"You're some doctor," he barely whispered. Oh, he wasn't improved. He was still delirious. Now he thought she was the doctor.

"Doctor Lisa," Teddy croaked and reached up for her fingers with his feverish hand. She was unable to utter a word so she kissed the top of his head. She wanted to express her great love but knew he'd scoff at her sentiment.

"Looks like you'll soon be running around chasing me again. Can't keep a wildcat down."

Painfully he managed a grimace. "Hurts to laugh."
Then Mama entered the room and insisted that Teddy go
to sleep. Shyly, blowing him a kiss as she had done when
they were toddlers, she retreated to the door, walking
backward until she could see him no longer.

5

The Midnight Raid

A MONTH LATER Teddy almost made Lisa cry again. "Oh, how can you be so absolutely horrible," she shouted at him.

"But I'm an invalid. You have to be *nice* to me and not upset me," he taunted. "Now where were we, teacher; ah, yes, the lesson on the British Empire. After Henry the Eighth there was Elizabeth, or was it Mary, Mary quite contrary?"

The doctor said Teddy had contracted a touch of rheumatic fever with his pneumonia and had to remain at home for at least a couple of months. Many of the children at school had come to see him the first weeks of his recovery. They had brought him gifts and tried to talk to him. But Teddy had been stubborn and sullen, although pleased to be the center of attention. He refused to be friendly with them, claiming that he would soon be moving again from this town and he wasn't going to get involved with anyone.

So gradually they had stopped visiting him, and now he was completely dependent on his sisters and brother. The others had gradually met friends and right now Lisa wanted to join Marion Brown outside instead of sitting here with her brother. But Teddy had told their mother that he must have Lisa with him.

"I just wish you were all recuperated and back in school so I could go out and play with my friends. Look at my arm. It's all bruises from when you threw that grammar book at me. I can't wait until you can go back to school. Instead of playing, here I am trying to help and amuse you and you're simply beastly to me . . ."

"Lisa, don't shout at your brother and upset him. You know what the doctor said," Mama's voice cautioned from the other room. It had been like this for the past two weeks. At first they were all delighted to nurse Teddy; do anything to bring back some flesh to his skinny frame and a smile to his face. But tutoring him now, Lisa was certain he was practically better and that he was torment-ing her only to relieve his boredom. He even made threats about running away from home when he was well again.

"I'm going to tell Mama that you always throw things at me and she'll let me leave you," Lisa threatened. "Be-sides, you have that wonderful set of books that Papa brought for us, and there's loads of games and things to make from that."

This remark brought a strange gleam to Teddy's eyes. He hesitated for a moment, then went racing for one of the thick red volumes of the children's encyclopedia. "Lisa, this book just gave me a great idea . . . but you've got to cross your heart, hope to die, and keep it a deep, deep secret."

Lisa hadn't seen Teddy this enthusiastic in months, and she became still more curious as he shut the living room door for privacy. Although she felt too adult for such gestures, she agreed to cross her heart, and for good measure, gave him their old secret handclasp.

"Now tell me."

He had the book marked with a bright piece of cardboard with the letter *P* on it. He tapped the book with his finger. "Here, young lady, lies the key to our future, our new world." Then he opened the book. "Puppets," he whispered as if this were a magic phrase like Open Sesame. Her face fell. What a disappointment.

"Lisa, Lisa, marionettes, wooden people who will do whatever we want. We'll have our own private friends to always play with. Even if Papa decided to move next month we'd still be able to take our friends with us. No more good-byes. Forget all the others. Just pack up the wooden people and we've left nobody behind."

She still felt reluctant to share his enthusiasm. "We couldn't even afford to buy any," she scoffed.

Irritated by her lack of vision, he tried to explain his ideas for he was determined that she should share his excitement. "No, no, look at the directions here in the book. We'll make our own puppets. Dozens of them. And they'll all be different characters. You can write plays for them to act in . . . you love writing stories."

"But where will we get the material to make them with?" She was beginning to share his excitement.

"Easy, the remnants bin in the store. We can collect all

sorts of junk here to make them out of, and no one can ever take them away from us. Better still, we can pack them up with us wherever we go no matter where Papa moves us."

As Lisa listened to him describe the marionettes and all the wonderful things they could make, the fairy-tale plays that the puppets could act out, the hours when Teddy could mold the heads and limbs, she found herself increasingly involved. She still tried to warn Teddy that puppets never would take the place of real people but he just shook his head. Teddy hadn't looked this happy since he was building the houseboat on the lake, and she saw no sense in discouraging his sudden enthusiasm.

Teddy undoubtedly would have loads of time to work on the puppets during the next few months. She thought to herself that the winters here were supposed to be long and cold. Marion had said that there might be weeks and weeks when they had to play in the house. She claimed that sometimes the temperatures here on the prairies dropped to forty below and the snow was so deep that it dwarfed an adult. Well, Marion must be a great one for making up whoppers, but still they'd have to spend a lot of time indoors when winter set in.

Teddy explained that they wouldn't make sissy hand puppets but wonderful ones that sang and danced, moving their legs and their arms. The book gave detailed instructions on how to construct such puppets.

"Shhhh. Listen at the door to make sure no one is eavesdropping and then put a chair in front of the door," he instructed.

"But, but . . . are you sure we're smart enough to make these marionettes?"

Teddy crossed the room. Slowly he opened the old chest of catalogues beside the piano and pulled out a large brown paper bag. He drew out a clumsy eighteen-inch puppet with a gigantic smile painted on his face, crinkly yellow hair that looked the color of Suzanne's old sweater, and bright red freckles. The puppet wore a crudely fashioned sack made from old overalls.

"Why hello there, Miss Lisa Stein. Nice to make your acquaintance. I'm Jack the Giant Killer." The wooden fingers shook the top of her hand and his legs, fastened to strings that joined to a rod in Teddy's hand, gave a merry skip. He was absolutely wonderful, and she threw her arms around the creature to give it a hug.

"Oh no, Lisa . . . you'll get the strings all mixed up." And sure enough, poor Jack collapsed in a pile of knotted strings. "I'm not much good at sewing," Teddy added.

"And now we must have a giant and his ugly wife," she replied. For the next two hours before dinner, they worked together as Teddy explained the process. First they needed clay or wood to mold a head and pieces of wood to make arms and legs and a body. All the parts were held together by loops of wire attached to string. The body was a simple wooden frame shaped with the arms fastened at one end and the legs at the other.

They fashioned a disgusting head of hair for the giant from rope remnants and soon the giant was ugly enough to inspire fear if not hatred. If only they could have painted a better face. His crossed eyes were acceptable but the crooked mouth was so wobbly that it almost made him a comic figure.

Jack lay lumpishly in the corner as they worked on creating the giant; it was almost as if Jack had a premonition that the grotesque figure they were constructing was indeed going to chase him down the beanstalk. Since Teddy was unable to leave their apartment, Lisa volunteered to go into the store every evening to collect odd pieces of fabric and wire to make the puppets. They agreed that their parents must never know about their new hobby.

"It's not that we're taking anything valuable from the store. It's only scraps that they'll throw out anyway. But Papa will say this is a waste of time — he hates plays — and Mama would tell Papa . . . besides, what fun would it be if it wasn't our own private world. Just our own secret?"

Lisa also thought it was stupid that Papa hated playacting so very much. However, she certainly wasn't going to discuss it with him right now. After much insistence Teddy had finally permitted her to invite Suzanne and Mike to be members of the wooden world they were creating. After all, Suzanne was the best person at sewing in the entire family; she spent hours with her sewing basket making dolls' clothes. The garments she fashioned looked like real clothes and not like the strange misshapen things Lisa tried to sew with her bumbly fingers.

A week later they made plans to enter the store secretly for extra materials. Teddy was determined that not even their mother should know anything about the puppet project.

"She'd tell Papa right away, and he'd rant at us about the dangers of the theater and that we'd all be ruined like old Aunt Ida. I can't stand the way he bosses us. Someday if he doesn't leave me alone I'm going to run away. Then let's see him give me a hiding."

"Shh, Teddy. Look, I got as many scraps as possible from the yard goods section. Told Mama I was making dolls' clothes. But now she wants to see the dresses I made so I can't use that excuse any longer," Suzanne said.

Many of the materials they required came from the hardware section of the store, and Lisa found it difficult to constantly manufacture excuses for entering this part of the building. Sweeping was the only chore she could think of and the clerk had jokingly asked her father if she wasn't planning to sweep even the customers out of the place with her constant puttering around there.

"Tonight's the night," Teddy had whispered. "Papa and Mama are going to the big charity Bingo at the community hall. They're bound to stay late since Mama loves Bingo, so we'll have loads of time to get everything we need while they're gone. Then we'll store everything in the attic."

Lisa hated to admit it but she was frightened. She had never entered the store at night and they couldn't risk putting on the lights while they foraged for their materials, since Macnamara would still be making nightly rounds. Teddy obviously had to stay upstairs. Mike proudly waved their only flashlight as they prepared for their raid. Suzanne giggled nervously as Teddy traced directions on the crude map of the store he had drawn during the afternoon.

"Gee, this is way more fun than run-sheep-run," Suzanne whispered. "With you for a leader, Captain Teddy, we'll be back here with everything before you even miss us."

Lisa wished she shared their enthusiasm.

Everything was blocked out on the map. Teddy had given them lists of specific items they were to find in various corners of the store when they split up in the warehouse. "More efficient that way," he explained, "and a lot less risk since it will be faster than moving around together." But, Lisa asked herself, how were they to find their way around the warehouse in the dark with its piles of barrels and boxes scattered helter-skelter all about the place? These crates were moved every day so they never could memorize their exact whereabouts.

Teddy glanced at his watch with the second hand, and motioned that the moment for action had arrived. Cautiously, the three children counted their way down the eighteen narrow steps to the warehouse. Mike had trouble with the flashlight. His hand was shaking and the beam darted this way and that. "My hands seem to shake all on their own," he complained as he tripped over a step. The floor creaked as they felt their way through the thick blackness. Lisa almost stumbled over a barrel of flour. "For goodness sakes, don't trip over the crates of eggs," she whispered.

All of them sighed with relief as they finally reached the entrance to the store itself. It was simpler to maneuver there because Papa always kept the bulbs in the display windows lighted. However, the lights also caused weird shadows to loom over the room, and Mike almost ruined the expedition when he squealed after an encounter with his own huge shadow.

Since it was close to Christmas, the shelves and tables were stocked high with piles of merchandise. Through the windows they caught glimpses of people trampling by, their footsteps muffled by the thick snow.

"Bet I'd make them jump out of their pants if I yelled boo," Mike said, as he peered invisibly behind a display at a man gazing intently in the window. Lisa told him that he was not to do any such thing but they were all less tense as they watched the world outside the big window. The three of them scattered in different directions to find the items on their lists.

Suzanne moved quietly to the back of the dry goods department for some cloth and snippings of crimson velvet to trim the robe of a queen. She had watched her mother folding merchandise that same morning, so she knew exactly where to look for the things on her list. Silver and gold cord were the major items on her list. No problem there.

Her youngest brother searched for balsa wood, wire, and glue, while Lisa pushed the big wooden ladder against the highest shelves so she could climb for a small can of special paint. In the semi-light she tottered on the ladder as she attempted to move a heavy can out of her way.

Fortunately Mike was close by and leaned against the ladder to prevent it from falling. "Just don't drop that can on my head," he whispered.

"I'll fall if I look down at you," she replied.

"So who asked you to look? Just go down one step at a time and don't dare look below."

It seemed to take hours for her to descend the shaking ladder but finally she was back on the floor with her paint cans clutched tightly in her arms. She didn't dare think what might have happened. Glancing at the alarm clock on the counter top, she realized that it was time to go back upstairs. With Mike's light they saw Suzanne motioning them from near the warehouse door. Rechecking their lists, they proceeded to the warehouse.

"Now wasn't that a snap," Lisa whispered, forgetting that she had been absolutely petrified a moment earlier.

At that moment a loud clattering suddenly echoed through every corner of the store. Like mice, they scampered behind a distant display counter. Panic-stricken, they held their breath. Suzanne hugged Lisa so tightly that she felt like a sardine in a tin. Mike was quaking behind her and his movements upset some metal washboards. Where did the noise come from? Who did it come from? What beast lurked in the blackness waiting to capture them? Another crash and it was simple to identify the source of the noise. The warehouse.

"What's in there?"

"A giant," Mike wailed.

"Some monster."

"Rats, huge field rats."

"Maybe a snarling wildcat. It moves so stealthily."

It could only be a burglar or a madman, a mean dark brute who would destroy all of them once he discovered their hiding place. A shuffling sound warned them that the monster was preparing to attack.

"Lisa, what will we do?"

"You'll be caught for sure if you make all that noise," a voice sputtered down the stairwell. Good gosh, Teddy obviously thought *they* had made the racket and now they heard him, hesitantly descending the stairs. Lisa tried desperately to think of some means to save her brother from the creature skulking near the bottom of the staircase.

The monster would grab their brother as soon as he entered the warehouse. He'd probably harm Teddy, who wasn't yet strong enough to escape. They had to do something besides cringing behind this counter. They had to defend Teddy. She thought of all the penny-dreadful magazines she had read. This sort of thing always happened in the pulp magazines, but she couldn't remember what the hero did.

Muffled footsteps warned her that IT was on the move again and either tracking them down or menacing Teddy. "Noise, make lots of noise, that's what we have to do. Let him think there are dozens of us and maybe he'll run away . . . at least it will warn Teddy."

The words were no sooner uttered than Mike banged on a copper boiler beside him. What a racket the hollow pot made! It would awaken the entire town. Suzanne crawled away and returned with two saucepans and clanged them together like cymbals. Lisa clutched the broom beside her.

"What on earth are you doing; you've got bats in your belfry. You've spoiled everything," Teddy shouted from above.

Covering her mouth with a hanky from her pocket, Lisa pretended she was the hero in the last silent movie she had seen in B.C. "Come out in the name of the law. We've got you," she squeaked. Wasn't that what the subtitles always said?

There was an unearthly wail from the warehouse. Again they froze. And Teddy, now aware that they were not alone in the store, stopped calling to them. The resulting silence was even creepier. If only Teddy had stayed up-stairs. The stillness gave her the heebie-jeebies, since their enemy might already be slipping closer. As if he had read her mind, Mike smashed his boiler again. They continued this racket like a band of madmen. Then they crept toward the staircase, ducking behind boxes for protection. Lisa

touched the case beside her cheek and felt the cold hardness of an egg.

"That's it, we'll pelt him with eggs." She reached for one and slowly it crunched in her hand as her fist involuntarily shut tightly at the sight that moved toward her. A great white ghost was wending its way across the room toward their hiding place. Like a creature from some other planet it swayed as it approached. The egg dripped down her arm to the floor but she still did not move. It was hopeless to fight this ghoul.

Suddenly an egg landed with a thump on the chest of the creature and immediately they all began pelting it. Still it moved closer and they prepared to run.

"What the devil is going on here? Stop, I say. I have a gun." Never had Papa's voice sounded stronger. Then he stepped in from the store with three other men. "Oh, Papa, save us," they all screamed.

The dripping white creature stopped and crumpled to the floor. Papa had killed him. Her father had actually killed something. Oh, how terrible. She covered Mike's eyes but Mike pushed her hand aside as he stared in solemn fascination at the heap before them. At that moment the lights went on and the men walked over to the creature huddled on the floor.

"Why, it's just old Jake Goodis, drunk as a skunk," one of the men said. "Poor guy's scared half out of his wits. Boy, you really must have ferocious kids, Stein. They really gave him a scare."

Papa had his arms around Suzanne and Mike by now. Sure enough, it was no burglar at all. And the white stuff that had made the intruder look so ghostlike was just plain old flour. He must have tripped over a barrel of flour, for they could now see gray heaps all over the warehouse. Neither Lisa nor Teddy dared say a word in case Papa started asking questions, but disappointment registered on both their faces.

"Hey, look back here, Mr. Stein," Macnamara shouted. "Somebody must have left this warehouse door unbolted. Not a sign of anyone forcing it. Old Jake must have just wandered in."

"Wait until I speak to my staff tomorrow," Papa replied. "Somebody will hear about this carelessness. Woke the whole town, frightened my kids out of their wits and wrecked the store." Papa turned as if to assure himself that they were unharmed.

"Those young kids of yours did a pretty darn good job of capturing him on their own. Hey kids, next time Macnamara needs to catch a thief, okay if we deputize you and call you in?"

Suzanne giggled and Mike imitated the way he would mow them down. Teddy and Lisa just grinned weakly, hoping that the two younger children would remember to keep quiet.

"Let's not get smart, children. And you have to go to school in the morning. Enough excitement for one evening. Just tramp up to bed, all of you. And next time, if you hear a noise, don't be heroes. Call me, call the patrolman, but don't you dare come down here yourselves or I'll give you a hiding."

Papa moved to the telephone so that the local operator could tell all the people on the party line that everything was fine. Papa always yelled into the phone, as if somehow he could cover the distance between himself and the unseen person at the other end by speaking very loud. When it was long distance he practically screamed and, during a local call, Mama was always shushing him and advising him to use his normal voice.

"You see, he doesn't even give us credit for catching the guy," Teddy grumbled as they brushed their teeth fifteen minutes later. "We're just nuisances to him, that's all."

"Oh come on, Teddy, he certainly looked concerned right after it happened," Lisa replied.

Teddy merely shrugged his shoulders. "Someday I'm going to run away from here, you'll see."

Lisa made a nasty face in response. Oh, it had been a thrilling time. She felt the goose pimples creeping down her arms as she recalled the dramatic evening. If only Papa and Teddy were friends. Well, perhaps if their puppets worked out, were successful, Papa might finally be pleased with Teddy. They had managed to hide their collection from the store and it would be easy to bring these things upstairs in the morning. But then, how to tell Papa about the puppets. He'd just throw them out . . . and . . . and she didn't dare think of the consequences . . . then Teddy would certainly leave.

6

Backstage in the City

LISA LOVED THE BREADTH OF the big city with the many tall buildings guarding the streets from the fury of the cold wind. How different this was from the barren openness of the prairie town where the people, not the elements, were the intruders. She pinched herself on this dull December day just to make sure she was finally here in Edmonton.

She still remembered her excitement when Papa had announced that, as a special treat, the family would go to Edmonton during Christmas vacation. They'd celebrate the holiday of Hanukkah, the festival of lights and dedication, with their city relatives. The children all loved this ancient Jewish festival, which coincided with their school holidays this year. On each of the eight nights of the event an additional candle was lit in a specially designed Hanukkah candelabrum, or "menorah."

"Oh goody, we can play the 'dreidel' game with spinning tops with lots of kids, and eat piles of yummy

potato pancakes at Auntie Sarah's, and get gifts of Hanukkah money," Mike had cheered when he heard the news.

During the festivities Lisa had felt a slight twinge of
sadness that poor Teddy had been forced to remain home
with Lucy. He had missed the huge dinner and the cere-
mony of lighting the beautiful brass eight-branched
menorah.

Now she was seeing the city with a distantly related
cousin, Ben Kahn, who had offered to show her around.
The gray-white dome of the Parliament buildings stood
silhouetted in the distance. The gaily colored streetcars
chirped along their frozen tracks while their bells clanged
loudly in the frosty winter air. The only horses in sight
were those pulling milk wagons. Her boots crunched firmly
on the packed snow as she lengthened her stride. Not the
hollow clump that came from the wooden plank sidewalks
of Chatko Falls, but a solid sound because here there was
real pavement under the snow.

She glanced at Ben, walking confidently beside her.
What a pleasure to discover some real cousins in the big
city! He was almost sixteen and quite handsome. He had
three older sisters and a younger brother.

"That was a wonderful ride on the streetcar," she told
Ben.

"You really are a strange girl, Lisa, getting a thrill from
a silly streetcar ride."

Blushing, she stopped to reply to this tall, blond boy.
Somehow she must explain her feelings to him. "But you
see, in the little towns where we've lived, there aren't any
streetcars, only horses and wagons and cars . . . and . . .
and tractors. Take the elevator at the department store.
Wow, we certainly don't have that in Chatko Falls. If Papa

doesn't carry a particular item somebody wants they can't buy it in another store but get it through the mail order catalogue. We don't have special wagons to deliver our milk or ice to keep the icebox cool. You take everything for granted here."

"Like what else?"

"Well." Lisa blushed but forced herself to continue. "Well, like a modern bathroom with running water and steam pipes to heat your home. Bet you never have to pile wood in your basement."

Ben nodded his head in agreement and put his arm around her shoulder. "You mustn't mind my teasing you, Lisa. Maybe it's because I've always lived in the city, but you make the country sound like more fun. I think sleighs are better than streetcars and when you talk about an open countryside for exploring . . ."

"I 'spose if you'd never tried it." Lisa sounded dubious. But what was it Papa always said? Something about the grass looking greener on the other side of the fence. Ben did live on the other side of the fence.

They were on their way to see the vaudeville show at the Pantages Theatre. Ben described the various acts he had seen last year when the traveling troupe came to the city and performed with some of the local players. The program the usher handed them as they entered the theater listed acrobats, a pantomime artist, tap dancers, singers, jugglers, ukulele players and even a play. The seats were almost full when they walked down the aisle.

"Did you know that girls often play the roles of boys in these plays?" Ben asked.

"Just the opposite to the plays in Shakespeare's times when men dressed as women," she replied.

"Hey, you're a rather smart girl for only thirteen. How did you know that?"

"Read about it. We have lots of time for reading at home, and besides, we're 'specially looking at books on the theater now because . . ." Oops, she had almost let their secret slip out.

Just then the orchestra began the opening chords of "God Save the King" and they stood with the other members of the audience. The show was fascinating. There was a group of World War One veterans who presented funny skits with several of the men dressed as women; four girls performed a rapid Charleston dance with the colorful fringes on their brief dresses flapping as they waved their hands in the air.

A magician drew rabbits, roses and silk scarves from his top hat, while two comedians followed a hefty tenor and a group of jugglers in satin and spangles. At the conclusion, Lisa's hands were sore from constant clapping.

"Oh, Ben, thank you so much for taking me even if I'm a mere thirteen. Didn't you feel like you were in another world, sort of on a different planet?"

"You say the strangest things. But you do seem older than your age. Hey, I'll bet you'd like to go backstage and get the actors' autographs."

"Can we really? Would they allow it?"

"I don't know if they actually encourage it but just follow me and we'll slip through the stage door before the caretaker catches us."

As the audience headed toward the lobby, they moved slowly forward, wedging themselves against the waves of people pushing in the opposite direction. He motioned her to duck down as they reached the front row of seats.

Crouched almost double, they raced behind the row, then slipped down the few steps through a curtain with a NO ADMITTANCE sign over it.

They walked down a dark aisle and up another set of steps. A man shouted something about flying something, and she turned to see the stage on her right, with a portion of the Arabian palace, being tugged into the air on ropes. A man knocked against them as he moved toward the stage. "Hey, what are you kids doing back here?"

Even Ben looked rather startled. "We'd like to get the actors' autographs," he whispered. The man paused for a moment.

"Well, I guess it's all right. But keep on going down to the left until you come to the blue door. Better knock before you enter." Neither of them moved.

"Oh, come on. I'll take you myself. Used to sneak back here when I was a kid, too." Mr. John, for that was the man's name, led them down several passages until he reached the blue door. Lisa noticed that he didn't bother knocking. They entered a warm room with big counters running the length of the entire wall. Long mirrors rested above the counters and dozens of players sat on chairs before the mirrors. Some were taking off their makeup, girls peered from behind screens where they stood changing their costumes, and several old gnomes, who had earlier appeared to be ancient men, were shedding their years as they removed beards and wiped off paint. The air was filled with a strange acrid odor. Lisa sniffed and Mr. John turned to her laughing.

"Greasepaint, that's what the actors put on their faces. Gets to you, doesn't it?"

"Where's the one who played the wizard in the play?"

Ben asked, looking around the room in disappointment.

Mr. John led them to the rear of the room, which was partitioned by curtains. "Stars have their own private dressing room. Hey there, Mr. Majunko, can I bring in a couple of kids who are your loyal fans?"

A deep husky voice answered the request in dignified tones. "Why certainly, bring them in, bring them in."

He was the strangest looking man Lisa had ever seen. He looked almost like the celluloid cupid doll she had at home. He had tightly curled white hair, and his face seemed a mass of baby pinkness with an upturned red nose and tiny mouth. His piercing green eyes were almost hidden below bushy red brows. Despite the cherubic face, he carried himself like a person of royalty.

"Like cat's eyes," Lisa said, then realized she had spoken aloud.

"Aren't you an observant young lady? Yes indeed, they are wild eyes, but very useful when you play a thousand different roles." He continued removing his makeup and applied cold cream as he talked. The huge upturned nose dropped off, and an ordinary straight one appeared underneath. "I use this one when I play the hero," he said, tapping his own nose. The pink tone gradually disappeared from his complexion and finally the bushy red brows also were removed. "Well, children, who would you like me to portray now?"

Ben asked if he'd mind being a villain again and Mr. Majunko raised his shoulders, narrowed his eyes, and growled in a menacing manner.

"Please, please could you show me how you change your voice," Lisa said.

"It's all from the diaphragm, all from down here," and

he pointed to his chest. "Just lots of practice. Why, I bet you want to be an actress, young lady."

She shook her head. "No, but I need to know about changing voices. I must have many voices."

Both Ben and Mr. Majunko looked puzzled. Oh, it was too great an opportunity for assistance to keep her secret any longer. She had promised Teddy not to tell anyone about their puppets but perhaps this man could help them.

"Well, well . . . Ben, do you promise not to tell a soul?" Ben nodded but still appeared startled. "Well, please, Mr. Majunko, do you know anything about marionettes?" Having uttered the fatal words, she decided there was nothing to lose by continuing. Then she told them all about the marionettes she and her family had made. "We've gotten fifteen finished now but we're having some trouble with their heads . . . and we don't know how to make a theater for them . . . and, well . . ." Her voice trailed off. "I know you think I'm foolish but I thought you might be able to give me some advice. Or maybe you know a book you'd recommend . . . I mean, aren't puppets sort of related to the theater?"

"Sort of related." Oh, now he was furious with her. What had she been thinking of, insulting him like this? But he continued talking. "Why, they're one of the first forms of theater man ever devised. There is absolutely nothing finer than a good marionette show." He continued talking about famous puppet theaters all over the world and the crowds that gathered to see the wonderful Punch and Judy shows in England. "Why, puppets are remarkable! Pity no one here ever seems to be interested in them."

Her shoulders sagged. "But you've come to absolutely the right place, young lady. In my homeland there are groups of puppeteers traveling all over the country. Do you know that the ancient Greeks and Romans had puppets? The Indians on this continent made a kind of puppet long before the white man ever landed here. And it so happens that during my youth I worked in a puppet theater."

Suddenly he seemed to have gone mad, for he rushed to the corner of his room where a great wooden chest stood. He threw dozens of items on the floor as he dug deeper into the huge box. First there was a crown, some fur-trimmed robes, then a scepter, two wigs and dozens of other items.

As he continued his search he mumbled incoherently to himself and Lisa could only shrug her shoulders at Ben. Ben put his finger to the side of his head and made a circle: "Bats in the belfry."

"My dear young man, there are no bats of any kind in this room," Mr. Majunko said in irritation. "Just be patient if you want me to help your charming young friend. . . . It has to be here . . . somewhere . . . never throw anything out . . . hahaaaaa . . . ahaaaa." Then, like a magician, he plucked a beautiful marionette from the bottomless chest. He gave a puff and blew dust off the most delicate face Lisa had ever seen.

It was a ballet dancer with deep auburn hair pulled back from her face and tied in a huge intricate bun. She had lovely kid arms which were so well-formed that it was difficult to believe there was need of the strings and rods from which she dangled. She wore a dainty, if crumpled, pink tutu and her shapely legs ended in pink toe shoes.

"Now my dear Christina, you must dance for these good

people," Mr. Majunko said, waving the wooden crossbar in the air and nimbly pulling the threads into their proper positions. "What's that you say? You're furious at me for having neglected you?" He bent his head toward the doll.

"Eet is impossible. You are a brute for having forgotten little Christina," a sharp falsetto voice scolded. "But they look as if they will have more appreciation for ballet. I shall dance the *Dying Swan* and you, my dears, please you will to forgive me if I am a little stiff at first. After all, such neglect, it has been years since I practiced my exercises at the *barre*."

Mr. Majunko allowed the marionette's feet to touch the dressing table. She gave a low curtsy. Her arms moved gracefully upward as she performed an arabesque, then she pivoted round and round on her pink slipper, gave a grand jeté, and finally stopped with a magnificent curtsy. She blew kisses at them. Lisa was so overwhelmed with the little dancer that she barely resisted embracing her. Hard to believe that it was only a puppet. Teddy was right. They could be real people. She noticed that Ben was also impressed with the dancer.

"Gosh, you make her seem just like a real person," he told Mr. Majunko. Then Lisa begged the actor to please teach her more about marionettes.

Once he learned that she wished to know how real marionettes worked, with rods and strings, rather than the simple hand puppets, he began to explain the many mechanical secrets that she could not possibly know. First he drew diagrams explaining the principles of movement in the limbs of the dolls. When properly constructed, a good puppet would have the ability to move its neck, wrists, fingers and knees by means of threading through wire loops in the various parts of the body.

"But how do you get those wonderful real faces?" Lisa asked.

"Papier-mâché is the most important ingredient." Then he showed her how a puppet head is created with properly shaped clay which is then hollowed out for the neck piece to fit in, with its various wires, not only at the bottom of the neck but through the ears. Then the clay is covered with papier-mâché strips; a mixture of wet paper, pasted on layer by layer and gently shaped until it has the right features on the clay. The nose, eyes and ears are fashioned to give the doll any special kind of appearance. Finally the papier-mâché head is left to dry, waterproofed with shellac when ready, and painted.

"Why, in our old studio we used to make dozens of heads at one time, always being careful to label them. Say, for example, a clown, or an old wizard or a beautiful young princess would all have different faces."

She clapped her hands together and couldn't resist giving him a big hug. "Oh, dear Mr. Majunko, you've been such a great help. Oh, I can already see so many different people . . . puppets that is. My brother Teddy will be delighted." Mr. Majunko smiled as he wrote down the name of a book she should borrow from the city library.

"My gosh, Lisa, we better get a rush on. Do you know what time it is? Mama will have kittens," Ben said.

"Good-bye, little kidlets, and do come and visit my shop whenever you need help with your puppets. I'd be delighted to give you any advice. I'm not always touring the road, you know." He wrote an address on a slip of paper and, as they were leaving, he stopped Lisa.

"Someone insists on going with you where she will truly have an opportunity to be famous," he said, handing the beautiful ballerina to her.

"Oh, oh but I couldn't . . ."

"But of course you can. You don't want a ballerina to be hidden in a trunk forever." He pushed the delicate doll into Lisa's arms. "Now I too must go and rest for tonight's performance." Before Lisa could refuse again, she was outside in the dim hall.

When they found their way to the exit they saw the snow falling gently. Lisa was startled to see the streetlights were already glimmering. What a great day, but here it was already evening.

"Lisa, you'll never find a streetcar that way. You have absolutely no sense of direction in the city. Come on, follow me." Ben led her around the corner, down two blocks, across a street and suddenly they were running for an approaching streetcar. Ben searched his pockets for a dime for the fare.

"Ben, you won't breathe a word to anyone, will you? Thank you for making this entire day perfect. And you will come to Chatko Falls and visit us? I can't promise it will be exciting like this but we may even have some good puppets for you to see by that time."

Ben gave her nose a slight tweak. "I've never met a girl with so many questions, nor one who has more fun. Of course I'll come and visit you, and you'd better hurry with your puppets because I'll be expecting a first-rate show when I arrive there."

7

Puppets in the Attic

SUZANNE PRESSED HER NOSE against the thickly frosted front window as she stared down at the main street of Chatko. School was closed this week because the roads were totally drifted in with six feet of heavy snow. It was so cold outside that the view was blurred by the thick coating of ice on the windowpanes. It was twenty-five degrees below zero, according to the thermometer outside the store, and the ice was even layered inside the window. The spot where her warm nose had rested a moment before was clear of frost, and she peeked through this opening with her eyes squinted, as if it were a keyhole.

"Well, has she gone yet?" Teddy called.

"You'll really lose your nose, it'll drop off if you keep pressing it to the ice like that, Suzanne," Lisa admonished.

They were all waiting to see if Mama had crossed the

street to the post office so that they could safely carry a huge bundle of puppets up to the attic.

"Yes, she just went inside, and my nose is fine. It feels so nice and cool; so hot being cooped up in here for so long . . . like an Eskimo." And then like a puppy, out flicked her narrow pink tongue and she licked the glass with it. "See how fast it refreezes, and your tongue sticks to it for a moment?"

"Come on, we've got to hurry or we'll never get all this stuff up there," Teddy answered. "And Lisa's right, you aren't a snake dependent on your tongue, it's a silly habit."

The four Stein children dashed to their various bedrooms, swiftly gathered puppets from under their beds, lifted boxes of materials stashed under beds and in closets. Within five minutes, a huge pile of precious belongings was sitting in the hall entrance to the apartment.

"You didn't forget the witch this time, did you? Can't have a play without her," Lisa said. "I wrote *Night in the Haunted Castle* especially for her . . . and oh yes, the little match girl . . . you know, the doll with the long tangled hair and the big sad eyes . . . she'll do perfectly for the heroine . . . you know, the one who gets trapped in the castle moat."

"Yes, yes, here she is, Lisa." Teddy produced the pitiful-looking creature from a pile of marionettes. "And I even finished the crocodile, to lunge at her from the waters. See, look at those huge teeth. Did you remember the blue cellophane for the water, Mike?"

They all talked rapidly as they stood beside the rickety ladder nailed against the wall, the only entrance leading to the attic. Teddy crawled up the rungs with his flashlight and opened the trapdoor. What an unbelievable find this room had been! Their collection of marionettes had grown rapidly—or had been born, as they all jokingly stated—since Lisa's trip to Edmonton. They had been delighted with the beautiful ballerina Lisa had brought home. The doll was like a challenge to them. It seemed to ask if they could provide her with similar friends, and they had shown great enthusiasm in making dolls to equal such grand company.

Lisa had written Mr. Majunko for more advice and Teddy had sent away for two books on marionettes. Their friendship with Tom Barker had been another stroke of luck.

"What an intricate face you've carved from that bar of soap. Isn't soap tricky to work with?" Lisa had said to Tom one recess as she watched him whittling. Tom Barker had blushed at the unexpected compliment. Two years older than Lisa, he was the son of a carpenter and skilled in working with wood.

"I bet you'd be fantastic with puppets."

Although he knew nothing about marionettes, he had learned quickly from the pictures Lisa brought him to copy. He was much better at making their movable joints than any of the others and could make the most difficult puppet move with grace. He was also able to provide all sorts of wood and wire from a never-ending supply.

What clever faces he made! Chubby baby faces, ugly rogues, handsome young heroes and all sorts of characters whom Lisa described to him. Even Teddy was polite to Tom now although he claimed that it was only a necessary arrangement since his sisters were awkward in this area. Just then there was a sharp knock on the back door.

"Must be Tom. Didn't think he'd come when it's so cold out and he has so far to walk. Quick, Suzanne, let him in before he freezes," Lisa called from her perch halfway up the ladder.

Suzanne gave the door a sharp pull and Tom practically tumbled in like a white snowman, with a miniature snowman right at his heels. Quickly he untied the red scarf protecting the face of the smaller boy with him. The long scarf was matted with gobs of snow.

"Sorry, but this is my kid brother Davey." Tom peered cautiously at Teddy, who scowled from the attic opening. "I — I know how you feel about strangers, but Teddy, Ma told me I had to mind him today and gee, he'll be our first real audience."

Lisa tightened her fingers on the rungs of the ladder as she waited to see what Teddy would do. Teddy still avoided other children. He would be returning to school as soon as the cold spell broke, but he refused to make any friends since he was certain that Papa planned to move once again in the summer. He and Papa rarely spoke to each other. The situation had been impossible since Papa had brought him those lovely presents from Edmonton.

Teddy had defiantly dropped them in the corner of the living room.

"I don't want your expensive presents. They can stay here and gather dust. I just wish we didn't have to be rolling stones. . . . Instead of gifts why don't you give us a real home we can dig our feet into?" he had asked.

Now Teddy's frown disappeared as he stared down at Tom. "Well, I 'spose it's all right if he promises to keep the secret. Guess it won't hurt. Now take your boots off before you have mud all over the floor or Mama will have

a fit." Teddy disappeared into the attic and they could
only hear him thumping above them as he moved around.

Like firemen passing buckets to put out a blaze, they
automatically assumed their places in the line going up the
ladder to the attic. The marionettes and materials passed
from the floor up to Mike and Teddy. Even Tom's brother
assisted without a word from anyone. Finally, when their
entire collection disappeared through the small opening,
they too climbed the ten rungs of the ladder and closed
the door behind them. At that point little Davey was
frightened.

"Wanna go home, Tom, wanna go home now, it's dark
up here and lots of spiders," he bawled.

"Shhh . . . no spiders here. Wait a minute and your
eyes will get used to the light. Don't you want to see the
play I told you about?" Tom said.

It was gloomy in the attic, but a stream of cool light
came through the two windows. They also had candles
stuck in bottles all around the floor and on overturned
wooden crates. Naturally Teddy, with so much free time
during his sickness, had been the first to discover the attic
door. There hadn't been a wooden ladder then. Teddy
also had the inspiration to turn the attic into the headquarters for their puppet theater. They had finally received permission from their parents to use the space.

Mama said she would be delighted not to have all their
strange garbage cluttering up the bedrooms. She also told
Papa that the children needed some place to play when the
weather took such drastic drops. Papa had even arranged
for the handyman to build the ladder against the wall.

Since the ladder was very steep no adult had ever
bothered to see what they kept in the attic itself. Even

Mama, with her mania for cleanliness, refused to trust the ladder. She explained that her bad varicose veins made the journey up the ladder impossible.

The room really looked cozy once the candles were lighted. They had built a rough stage out of cheese crates with stout beams nailed to the two ends of the boxes and a third beam nailed across the top. A curtain of burlap sacks hid the puppeteers from any audience they might have. Although it was a pity that they were unable to erase the stenciled potato labels from the burlap, it still resembled a real stage.

"Do you know that Lisa just finished writing our fourteenth play," Suzanne proudly told Tom. *"The Haunted Castle* will be the best yet. I don't know where she gets all her ideas."

Teddy, who directed the puppeteers, was also the most talented actor. He helped all of them create voices for the dolls they handled, but his puppets were always the most convincing. Lisa didn't quite know how he managed it, but his range of voices was unbelievable. His dolls always seemed more alive than those operated by the others.

Perhaps it was because Teddy treated them like real people. Suzanne was good with the puppets too, but you could always tell that it was just a game with Suzanne. When Teddy put a puppet away it was as if he were putting a baby to bed.

Lisa watched Teddy carefully choosing puppets for the new play. "Now, Mike, you'll tear off his arm if you pick him up like that. Have a little respect . . . you think he's just a block of wood?" Tenderly, Teddy lifted the silver knight for Mike. The silver knight was really one of their most successful creations. His armor was made of the tops of tin cans, bottle tops and silver paper. He clanked and rattled as Mike raised his arms by their strings.

Then Teddy handed the match girl to Suzanne, the crocodile to Tom, the mother to Lisa. Only he could be trusted to act the roles of both the wizard and his servant. Amazing how Teddy handled two puppets! The entire family was now capable of pretending to be different characters but only Teddy was always totally convincing.

"Why do you always get the villain?" Suzanne complained. "Even the witches. Listen to my voice." She gave a low cackle. "Isn't this good? I'm going to feed you to my hungry crocodile, little girl, he's waiting for his meal."

They choked with laughter. Suzanne had such a high voice that it sounded like an old rooster when she tried to change it. "I wanna go home . . . now," Davey wailed.

While Tom wiped the tears from Davey's face they all prepared quickly for their play. Lisa handed out carefully written lines to the various actors. There was a special tension in the air since Davey, young though he was, was their very first audience.

Lisa had hoped their cousin Ben might be the first to view the theater. She wrote to him every week and twice they had made arrangements for him to visit Chatko Falls. Frequent snowstorms had always prevented his visits, however, and Ben's father had finally decided that any trips must be postponed until springtime. It was true that the blizzards really did sweep down on their small valley with great suddenness. Once this winter they had been cut off from the outside world for a week until the heavy road cutter made it through.

"Lisa, you're on, Lisa, are you daydreaming or something?" Teddy hissed.

"Oh, where can my poor little daughter be?" she said, meanwhile manipulating the strings and rods of the mother's arms so that the hands covered the doll's face. "I told her never to go near the terrible castle of Greenhaven Glen, for there is a darkly dangerous monster lurking in the moat . . ." and so the play moved ahead. For a first reading it really went very smoothly. Suzanne's heroine shrieked and gasped as the enchanted crocodile attempted to pull her under the water. The knight, who had trouble with his sword, finally beat the wicked wizard.

"It was wonderful, wonderful. Oh so much better than anything in the world," a voice shouted. Claps of applause followed. "Best thing I ever did see. Get that horrible old wizard, get him." Little Davey really had enjoyed the play. Maybe they weren't so bad after all.

At ten o'clock the following morning Lisa was assisting Teddy with his homework. Since it was Saturday, Mama had gone downstairs to help at the grocery counter. They heard a sharp knocking and many voices at the back door.

"It's coming from the outside stairway. Didn't know Tom was coming this early," Teddy said.

"Lisa, please come out here right away and tell these stupid kids they're crazy," Lucy called. "Eight, twelve kids lined up there on the outside steps, crazy kids, say they've come to see a show."

"Must be a mistake," Lisa gasped. "Just let them pound, don't allow them in," she mumbled.

"Now look here, Lisa, I've seen some mighty funny goings on hereabouts and I ain't said nothin' to your ma, but I got work to do. Just you go out there and tell them kids yourself or I'm marchin' right downstairs and gettin' your ma up here." Lucy slammed a cupboard door to emphasize her remark.

Lisa and Teddy both rushed down the hall to the back door. They were shocked at what they saw through the tiny window. The pounding began again. Lisa was so frightened that Lucy'd call their mother that she finally opened the door slightly. There, true enough, lined almost all the way down the staircase to the back alley, were several children from the school. They all waved to her and shouted her name as she peered through the door. The boy who had knocked introduced himself. "I'm Willy George and we've come to see the puppet show."

"Don't know what you're talking about," Lisa mumbled.

"We got our money and we want to see them," shouted someone else waving a fist full of pennies.

"Hear *The Haunted Castle* is a real humdinger," another voice shouted.

"Oh, Teddy, what will we do?"

"Tell them to scram, right now."

"Davey says you do too put on plays and we come to see," Willy George said once again.

"Mama and Papa will hear them if they keep on shouting," Lisa whispered to Teddy. "Oh, and now they're stamping on the stairs."

"We want the puppets, we want the puppets," the voices began. Lisa was certain the stamping of heavy boots on the stairs would cause the entire staircase to collapse. Especially with all the heavy snow on it. Shivering in the doorway, she noticed that one man had already stopped in the alley and was staring up at the children to see what was causing all the noise.

"It's about time someone saw our marionettes. It was just plain old selfish to keep them to ourselves," Suzanne said from behind them. Teddy grabbed her by the shoulders and started shaking her.

"So you are the traitor, you were the blabbermouth, eh, spoiling everything."

There was only one thing to do if they didn't want to lose their puppets altogether. Lisa was relieved to see Tom dashing up the steps to assist her.

"Sorry, Lisa, I didn't know Davey would blab."

"You can come in, all of you, if you do so very quietly. You must keep this performance a secret. Now drop your boots here in the doorway and follow . . . follow the ushers up this ladder to the attic, I mean mezzanine," Lisa said.

Teddy had let go of Suzanne's trembling shoulders to listen. "I refuse, I will not allow it."

"Would you rather Papa found out and took the puppets away altogether?" Practical little Mike was already scattering newspapers in the hall for the boots. Teddy gave Lisa a strange challenging look, then headed up the attic ladder.

A half hour later the audience was settled on the floor or on boxes around the stage. Lisa was amazed that the kids were so quiet. They were never like this when they came to the special movies in the community hall. Teddy darted all over the room, giving directions.

"You did it, now it's your responsibility to entertain these kids," he hissed. "Don't forget your lines, Mike. Straighten out this little string that's caught on the clown here, Tom. Don't be a ham actress, Suzanne. You wanted to show off how good you are; now don't spoil it."

Maybe Teddy wasn't furious with her after all. He had

organized their troupe once the kids had found seats. At that point Lisa had gone absolutely blank. She had a dry sensation in her mouth and her fingers shook. She couldn't remember a line from a play, even though she had written all the plays.

"Now remember, if you flub a line, improvise. That means to make up some other good words, Mike . . . and go on . . . no matter what happens, that's the most important thing. We'll have the little clown welcome the audience. Then we'll give them two plays. Let's see . . . which wooden people are handy?"

He glanced around the room and then chose *The Haunted Castle* and *Rumpelstiltskin* because everyone knew *Rumpelstiltskin* and Teddy reasoned that if anything went wrong the audience could still figure out the plot. They all stared at him silently. Suzanne's hand, clutching the rods of her puppet, started shaking. Tom, who was supposed to open the show with the clown, didn't move. He just stood there until Teddy relieved him of the doll and moved the tiny performer onto the stage himself.

Somehow they all managed to get through the first play. Oh, there were several pauses and mistakes. Lisa's puppet had gotten tangled with Mike's. Suzanne had missed a cue from Mike telling her to bring the match girl onstage. But she finally remembered. The one thing they weren't prepared for was the applause, whistling and stamping that greeted them. The audience loved the play and screamed for more.

With a greater sense of security they began their performance of *Rumpelstiltskin*. At all times it was Teddy who gave them confidence to continue. He whispered forgotten words into their ears. He picked up cues and at one point he improvised the funniest dance for his Rumpelstiltskin doll.

"Omigosh, Teddy, we've got to finish the play right away. Now." Lisa whispered in his ear as she moved her doll off the stage. She pushed her watch in his face to show him that it was past noon. Mama would be up any second to prepare lunch. "We've just got to get rid of these kids before she comes."

Furious, Teddy glared back at her as if to say that she had caused this situation and now it was up to her to get them out of it. He was so involved in the action of the play that he couldn't stop now. So instead they went faster. They fired their lines back and forth as the heroine tried to guess Rumpelstiltskin's name. The puppets darted across the stage like characters in a speeded-up movie. Sometimes the marionettes accidentally collided as the puppeteers rushed to beat Mama's arrival. This made the audience stamp the floor in delight. Instead of falling through the floor at the conclusion, Rumpelstiltskin keeled over briefly, then flew like a birdman across the stage, crashing into the wings. It was finally over. The audience clapped and whistled.

"Hooray for the best show in town," someone shouted.

"Now you all must leave, yes, yes, we'll have another performance next week," Lisa agreed. Anything to get rid of them fast. As she dragged the first child toward the steps a voice called up to her.

"Lisa, Lisaaaa, what is going on up there? Sounds like a stampeding herd of cattle. Lisa, come down here this instant."

Lisa bent over the trapdoor. "Just some kids over to play, Mama."

"Kids? Sounded like horses."

"They all wanted to see Teddy and we got to playing, playing games," Lisa continued. Wouldn't someone help her, do something?

Mama's frown disappeared. "Ah, in this cold weather they came all this way to see my Teddy. Oh, that's nice, very nice."

Lisa had found the right excuse. Mama always worried so much about Teddy and wanted him to have friends. She heard Teddy choking behind her and pushed him with her elbow.

"But such noisy games, Lisa?" Mama continued.

Lisa motioned for Suzanne and Tom to start sending the kids down the ladder. Perhaps Mama was satisfied now and would go back to the kitchen. Quickly the kids crawled down the ladder. Mama paid little attention to the first few backsides scampering out of her sight. "Zeke Perkins's girl, aren't you?" she asked one child. "Ah, the dress-maker's boy and three, five, seven . . ." Mama was beginning as one child after another slid out of sight. Lisa thought they'd never stop coming. It was like the old woman who lived in a shoe.

"Lisa, they're coming out of the walls maybe."

"All to see Teddy, Mama." She felt she was telling the truth, for Teddy undoubtedly had been the star performer today. Finally the last child had tugged on his boots and slammed the back door. Mama stood there as her other three children appeared. "My Teddy, so many friends you have, and here I was worried. This should really make you feel better, such popularity." Again Mama shook her head. "Wait until Papa hears about this."

8

Watch Your Tongue, Suzanne

B Y EARLY MARCH every pupil in the school spoke to the Stein children. Their marionette theater was no longer a secret and although they limited their shows to five guests at a time, so that Mama wouldn't become suspicious, there was always a waiting line of customers on Saturday mornings. Teddy grudgingly admitted that all of them had become very popular with their classmates. For despite a thaw in the weather the doctor said that Teddy still wasn't ready for school.

Now that the weather had improved slightly, Chatko Falls wasn't a half bad place to live. They'd walk together to the vacant lot at the end of the block and Teddy watched while his younger sister and brother joined in a spirited game of "Fox and Geese." They'd seen the game before but called it "Pie," since the playing field was actually shaped like a giant pie. The children would shape a huge circle in the snowy field, then bisect it into halves and quarters with the center being "home base." They spent hours with the fox attempting to tag all the geese, running breathlessly around the spokes of the circle.

Another pleasure of their small town in winter was the sleighs the inhabitants used regularly since the rural roads were too rough to make cars very practical. Even Teddy was bundled up in blankets and a thick bed of straw for invigorating rides in the sleighs. The jingling of the bells on the horses' harnesses made winter a most special season in Chatko.

One cold morning Lisa was helping Mama give Mike a bath when some of the children arrived at the door. "I can't come out and you can't come in, Mike's in the tub and he'll catch a draft if you open the door," she shouted. "Wait downstairs, Marion."

"Okay, Lisa, but remember to bring your skates when you're ready. They've finally cleared the skating rink."

"Darned bath. Now Mama will make me stay in the house all day so that I don't risk getting a chill," Mike said. "Hate baths. Don't see why we have to take them. Joey says his mom doesn't make 'em have a bath 'cept in the summer . . . not healthy to have too many baths. Drains out all your strength."

Mama laughed as she handed Mike the huge bar of castile soap. "Lucy," she called, "fill the stove with some more coal and a few pieces of kindling. Then give it a poke. Please make sure that the doormat is stuffed right against the bottom of the back door. Don't want any drafts to reach him."

In the middle of the linoleum kitchen floor, resting on a

scattered pile of newspapers, was the huge tub. Mike's head
was barely visible above the top. He was still small enough
that he didn't have to scrunch up his knees to fit in. Lisa
and Mama had spent twenty minutes filling the tub with
boiling water from the kettle on the stove. On days like
this their mother longed for the running water available
in a big city. Teddy had taken his bath before Lisa's arrival
and now Mike was almost finished.

"No more hot water," Mike begged as Mama returned
to the stove for yet another kettle. "When you put it in
here the bottom of the tub gets like a pile of hot coals and
I burn my . . ."

Mama put her hand across Mike's mouth and the other
words were lost. "Lisa, go get some more snow in the
bucket so I can wash his hair," she said.

Gathering snow from the barrel on the back landing,
Lisa wondered why Mama insisted on special water for
washing hair. Always snow to melt for soft water, and in
the summer they were allowed to use only the water from
the rain barrel. As if hair couldn't be washed in the hard
water from the pump. But Mama had a special thing about
water. She claimed that hard water was the best kind for
drinking, full of minerals or something, and soft for
bathing.

Suzanne was in the kitchen when Lisa returned. Slyly
cupping a fistful of snow from the bucket, Suzanne let it
slip down Mike's bare back. He gave a great yelp as the
slippery snow melted down his shoulders, then flung himself into the air, splashing water in every direction. Mama's
crisp dress was soaked with suds, and rivulets of water
raced across the sodden newspaper and over the polished
floor. Lisa, who had been adding more sticks of wood to

the stove, was only slightly sprinkled but Suzanne was drenched too.

"Just look what you've done, look at this kitchen . . . and me. A terrible thing to do to your baby brother," Mama shouted at Suzanne. Mike had grabbed the huge bath towel on the kitchen chair and was taking advantage of this opportunity to escape from the room.

"Young lady, not only will you wash this floor but I forbid you to go to the skating rink with Lisa," Mama continued, mopping the floor as she spoke. "And you are also forbidden to go up for that attic nonsense with Teddy for the entire week."

"But Mama, it's almost twenty above zero outside and the first decent day for skating that we've had in weeks . . . oh, Mama, it was only a joke."

"Never mind, miss, this is your punishment. Enough talking. You can leave now, Lisa, since Mike's already disappeared. Poor baby, he could have heart failure from the way you frightened him, Suzanne."

"I'll get even for this, just you see, get even with all of you," Suzanne muttered as she slammed the door, searching for rags to sponge up the soapy water.

Two hours later Lisa remembered her sister's threat as she herself sat on a wooden bench beside the skating rink. The ice was rather pebbly and bumpy in spots, but what a pleasure to be outdoors after being stuck in the house for so long! And to be with a friend like Marion. Marion was as blond as Lisa was dark. Her ashen hair hung down her shoulders in two thick braids.

Days when the temperature made it impossible to take part in outdoor sports the two girls found new hobbies. Sometimes they made silhouette pictures of india ink on squares of glass and glued colored foil paper behind them. Their drawings were usually of beautiful ladies in hoop skirts or nursery rhymes copied from old books.

Marion had even taught Lisa how to make pot holders, aprons and pen wipers on the sewing machine. Lisa found the treadle pedal on the machine difficult to manipulate smoothly with her feet and it often ran away with her and her crooked sewing. While she wasn't really talented in sewing she appreciated the fact that Marion never laughed at her awkward efforts.

"Lisa, you're wool-gathering again," Marion teased, waking Lisa from these thoughts. Lisa described the unpleasant incident of Suzanne and her mother.

Marion thought the story was funny. "Gee, I wish I had a big family like yours. You do so many things together . . . like your puppet theater. Even your parents seem interested in all your activities. And they always care about where you're at and what you're doing."

"That's a strange thing to say, Marion. Who wants their parents butting in on everything? It's hard to keep any secrets in our home." Lisa shook her head in chagrin.

"Wish somebody'd notice whether I'm home. Dad always stays late at the shop and Mother at the post office." Marion paused.

"But we're always moving from place to place. Sure Papa is good to us, but we just never settle anywhere, a new town almost every year."

"Gee, I think that'd be nice. I was born here in Chatko right in the same house where we live now. Went to Edmonton once to see the Highland Games and will probably live here forever and ever like Gramps. Boy, I sure wish my parents wanted to travel. Never even been south in the province to Calgary; I'd love to see their Stampede someday, never mind the rest of the world. I think your dad's nice. Gee, I remember the night he was telling you that story, he's a great storyteller."

Lisa didn't wish to pursue the discussion. She wasn't in the mood to hear her father's praises sung. The sun was still glowing down on the rink but it wouldn't remain much longer in March. She finished tying her skate, stamped her foot to make sure it was tight enough, then motioned for Marion to join her on the ice.

The rink was circled by low wooden walls with the only changing room being a lean-to shack on the edge of the ice. Since the frame fence was so low the snow constantly drifted over the fence onto the ice, making it impossible to sweep the ice clean on windy days. The ice was marked with red and blue lines for hockey and the goals stood at either end of the rink. Since this was free skating time only a few younger boys were practicing shooting pucks into the goals.

A long line of shouting kids, their hands tightly joined, came rushing down the ice. She watched the anchor man suddenly stop, dipping to the side and digging in his skates while the rest of the line flipped far out in a great cracking motion, like a line of birds changing direction in the sky. "Crack the Whip" was her favorite ice game besides "Pom-Pom-Pullaway," and she glided across the ice to where several giggling kids, the tail end of the whip, lay strewn on the ice. It took courage to be on the end of the whip, for this was where the momentum of the crack would be strongest. The girls joined the whip for a while and then the music of a Strauss waltz floated in the air from the old Victrola by the bench.

"Oh good, some music. They've finally fixed that old thing. Let's cross arms and skate together. I just got my skates sharpened." Marion took a quick turn around the rink, and sharply reversing the blades of her skates, she stopped abruptly beside Lisa, the honed blades sending slivers of ice and snow in Lisa's face.

"Gee, I wish Papa would get me speed skates like those," Lisa said admiringly. They joined arms and circled round the rink enjoying the sharp even cutting sound as their skates touched the ice in unison. At one point Lisa thought she saw Suzanne standing in the shadows behind the shack but when she skated over there she decided it had been her imagination. The spot was empty. When they finally entered the skating house and took off their skates beside the pot-bellied little stove, they had tears in their eyes. The temperature had dropped several degrees, and their feet, bound so tightly in the boots, had become numb from the cold despite extra layers of socks. Tugging at the stiff waxy lace of her second skate, Lisa felt her feet beginning to thaw. She hopped around the room like a kangaroo as she tried to improve her circulation. As sensation returned to their toes the girls both felt thousands of prickles bite into their feet. They were too wise to put their feet near the stove at this stage. Circulation had to return slowly or the pain would be unbearable, so they sat and rubbed the thick socks until their feet felt as if they were burning.

"The temperature really must have dropped outside," Marion said, looking vainly at the large broken thermometer hanging outside the door. "My dad says that if your feet really get too frostbitten, you should rub them in snow to bring back the circulation."

"Omigosh, I almost forgot," Lisa gulped. "I promised Mama I'd pump a pail of water from the Christopher well."

"But you have a pump of your own right behind the house," Marion replied as they tied their skates together and threw them over their shoulders.

"You know that and I know that but Christophers' is the only soft-water well in town and Mama's got a thing about soft water." The girls shook their heads as they hurried down the back lanes toward the well. Adults were peculiar about some things. They stopped at the foot of the Stein back staircase, where the tin pail stood waiting.

"I'll walk you over to the well since it's almost on my way," Marion offered. En route they paused by a fresh patch of snow. It was absolutely smooth and glassy — not even a dog's print marred the surface. With their hands tightly at their sides, they leaned backwards and flopped onto the new snow. Lying flat on their backs, they raised their arms up to their shoulders as if they were performing some sort of ritual exercise on their backs. They arose cautiously so that they would not disturb their patterns on the snow and studied the "angels" they had fashioned. "See," Marion pointed, "mine looks as if she is a princess with a crown."

"And mine looks like a great jolly clown," said Lisa, studying the silhouettes a moment longer.

"I hate going to Christophers' pump, 'specially if I have to carry two pails. Teddy used to do it but now I'm stuck with his chores."

In the summer months it was a plain ordinary red steel pump, and quite easy to handle. But whoever had originally chosen the site for the pump had mistakenly built it on the top of a small hill. In the winter, the excess water dripping over the rims of the pails gradually built into a steep slope of ice so that after one had filled a bucket, the big trick was to cautiously creep down the slippery mound without falling. On more than one occasion Lisa had slipped and found herself, bruised and wet, at the bottom of the slight hill with her overturned pail resting by her feet. She was sure that Jack of the nursery rhyme must have suffered his own crown-smashing experience on a similar hill.

Turning the final corner to the well, they saw someone at the summit of the ice cone. "Guess we'll have to wait a few minutes. There's someone at the pump," Marion said.

"Hey, that looks like Suzanne, sure it is. Do you think Mama got impatient and sent her ahead?" She waved to Suzanne but her younger sister did not turn around. She merely waved one arm in a rather jerky motion.

"Gee, she must still be angry about her punishment. She won't even turn around to speak to you," Marion whispered as they carefully sidestepped their way up the ice hill. Ever-widening circles of bumpy ice had built on the hill and the girls did not stop to look at Suzanne as they concentrated on maneuvering up the slope.

"Suzanne, whatever are you doing?" Lisa shouted when they reached the summit. "You don't even have a pail. Oh, come on, Sue, don't be so stubborn. Talk to us. It wasn't my fault."

But Suzanne wouldn't talk. She merely flailed both arms in the air like a beserk windmill and kept her face pressed against the pump.

"Omigosh, she's licking the pump," gasped Marion.

"Suzanne, I told you not to stick your tongue on things

like frozen pumps . . . it's silly. Now let go and let me get my chore done." But Suzanne just stood there and motioned to the pump with one fuzzy blue mitten. Only then did Lisa realize that Suzanne had her tongue firmly attached to the pump. There was a long pause.

"How long have you been here?"

Suzanne turned her wide blue eyes toward them in a beseeching gesture. Rapidly she opened and closed her fist to show the passage of time.

"A half hour! Oh, Suzanne! Have you really tugged hard to get it off? You'd only lose a little bit of skin off your tongue, you know." Lisa tugged at Suzanne's shoulders, then stopped. She was frightened that she'd tear out her sister's tongue if she did so.

Suzanne didn't dare shake her head. She pressed her mittens to the sides of her face in her favorite woe-is-me gesture and then tears began dribbling down her cheeks.

"Oh, Suzanne, we'll get help. Don't cry. You'll freeze your face." Now it was obvious that it wasn't just the tip of Suzanne's tongue that was glued to the pump but the entire soft upper surface. Rapidly, she directed Marion to remain at the pump. Neither of the two older girls needed to discuss the fact that Suzanne would freeze if she remained still much longer. Unable to move even a few inches, Suzanne could not keep the frost from invading her limbs. Lisa undid her wool jacket and threw it over her sister's shoulders.

"Rub her back and arms while I get some help," she yelled to Marion as she skidded down the slope.

A few minutes later Lisa burst through the front door of Papa's store. There were many customers waiting but she pushed past them in search of her father. Finally she spotted him in a corner, counting out eggs for a customer. "Oh, Papa, come quick, get the police, get someone. Suzanne is stuck to the Christopher pump and we can't get her off."

Papa stared at her as if she was a raving maniac and she blurted out the entire story. "It just isn't possible," Papa replied. The customers stood around laughing but Papa must have realized that there was no such word as impossible in the Stein vocabulary for he immediately reached for his coat on a nearby hook.

"It isn't funny. She'll freeze to death if we don't get her tongue off the pump," Lisa shrieked at the bystanders.

She found it difficult to keep up with Papa as he ran down the street looking for the constable. She supposed someone would remember to call Mama from upstairs. There sure was a big group of people following them as they rushed toward the well. Everybody seemed to think that there was something humorous about the incident. Suzanne stood shivering by the pump as the crowd rushed to the foot of the ice hill. She looked as if she would faint when she saw the curiosity-seekers climbing toward her. Several of the men carried shovels with different-shaped blades. One man even had a hatchet and another clutched a garden trowel and fork.

Papa shouted for most of them to stay at the bottom of the hill since the top, where the pump stood, was very narrow. Suzanne's blotched cheeks turned a bright crimson, then her eyes almost popped out of their sockets when Papa directed the first shovel at a point directly below her tongue.

"Oh, my poor baby, you'll kill her," Mama called. Obviously someone had told Mama too.

"Don't worry, little one, we're not going to hurt you," Papa told Suzanne but his voice sounded shaky. The men took turns trying to maneuver narrower blades under her tongue. To do this they had to crouch awkwardly on the brow of the hill. "It just won't work," Papa said.

One of the men handed Papa a heated dull table knife. Suzanne's arms flopped about rigidly, like one of their puppets, and her tears began spilling down again. Delicately Papa maneuvered the warmed knife against her tongue but it still wouldn't budge.

"Hey Stein, it's going to drop to twenty degrees below zero tonight. You've got to do something to get her off that darned thing. Maybe we could tear out the pump before she freezes to death," the town banker warned.

The postmaster shouted that she'd lose her tongue altogether if they handled her roughly and someone else said that was better than freezing to death. Lisa wished he'd shut his mouth. Now Suzanne could barely stand, even with her mother's arms pressed tightly around her.

"Get a doctor from the next town."

"She's going to be mute for sure."

"Tear down the pump and carry them both home."

While half of the town shouted advice, the town drayman rounded the corner with his sleigh and horses. Someone stopped him and suggested he try to pull out the pump. He climbed the hill toward Suzanne and then hesitantly made a suggestion. "Why don't you heat the pump? Only thing to do. Thaw it."

"Now why didn't I think of that," Papa muttered, slapping his bald head. "Thank you, Mr. Wirkowski."

"A blowtorch, that should do it." Several men raced away from the hill to fetch one. By the time they returned with the blowtorch most of the town stood gathered at the bottom of the ice cone. They all stared up into the gathering dusk as if they had sighted the messiah or an eighth wonder of the world. Mama tightened her grasp on Suzanne's mitten. Teddy whispered encouragement from the bottom of the hill. Suzanne closed her eyes as the flame from the blowtorch drew closer. Mike began to whimper as if the tool was being aimed at him.

What if they burned Suzanne on this icy pyre like Joan of Arc on her pile of wood? And indeed the crowd of onlookers could have been the French townspeople gathered to see a witch-burning. They appeared excited rather than frightened. Lisa could bear it no longer and also shut her eyes. If only she knew an appropriate prayer or if she had her rabbit's foot in her pocket for good luck.

The smell of the acrid torch pierced Lisa's nostrils and she coughed.

"That's it, boys, the ice is melting, it's warming."

"Heat it but for God's sakes don't let it get too hot or you'll burn the kid."

The men took turns holding the torch closer to the round belly of the innocent pump. Suddenly Suzanne gave a muffled wail and fell back into Mama's arms. Her tongue was finally free. Everyone let out a great whoop of victory.

"We've done it."

"Maybe she'll even be able to speak again."

"Say something, my little sheep," Mama said. Suzanne, her eyes cast downward, could only lean against Mama.

"Aaaahhhh," she gurgled. Then Papa swooped her up and carried her down the hill, with the entire town following close behind him until they finally reached the store.

9

Talent Night Announced

WHEN SUZANNE RETURNED to school she was treated as if she were some kind of celebrity. All the kids wanted to play with her, hear about her experience at the pump and, above all, stare at the famous tongue. A reporter had even come down from Edmonton to interview her and he had brought a photographer with him. Someone said that it was the kind of story that would reach Ripley's "Believe It or Not." Papa just said he'd rather believe it was all a bad dream and that they'd all better keep out of trouble and avoid such monkey business in the future. Mama wanted to know how her children could get into such incredible mischief; Teddy, who had returned to school, suggested Suzanne should lick a few more frozen metal objects if it resulted in her having to forgo conversation for a solid month at a time.

Spring came late to Chatko Falls. Mama claimed that in British Columbia the tulips and daffodils were already in full bloom by March. Lisa was satisfied that the blizzardy, below-zero weather had almost disappeared by mid-April and that the snow was gradually melting. You could even see green buds on some of the trees and more birds arrived each day. On especially warm days they could abandon their galoshes for high rubber boots. What a pleasure it was to deliberately slush through the thinly coated ice puddles and feel them crack under the boots and finally give way.

"Just think, Marion, in a couple more weeks we'll be able to wear knee socks." Lisa detested the heavy woolen stockings and itchy fleece underwear she was forced to wear on the prairies in the winter. The thick one-piece undergarments always created extra bumps and creases in her clothing and made her look like an elderly lady.

Marion nodded from her desk across the aisle but Lisa saw that she already had prepared for spring by rolling her stockings down over her knees. Mama never allowed that and Lisa never quite dared to disobey her for Mama was certain to find out some way.

"Shhhhh," Marion whispered from behind her exercise book, "Mrs. Beddlington is going to tell us about the Easter concert."

Mrs. Beddlington was pounding on her desk with a ruler to get their attention. This new teacher was young and always had different and unusual projects for them to do during Social Studies and Science.

"Now class, we have a bit of a problem regarding our Easter concert this year. Miss Jones always made advance plans so that you could learn which poems to prepare and recite for the pageant. Since she took sick I'm afraid we've had our hands full just keeping up with the curriculum, so I just didn't get around to handing out recitations . . ."

"Hooray," Teddy whispered from behind Lisa. "Hate those horrible dull poems . . . always the same pap. Dozens of nothing lines to memorize. Guck, real guck."

"Teddy Stein, did you have a suggestion you'd like to offer to the class?"

"No, Mrs. Beddlington, nothing, just mumbling to myself."

"Then, if you have nothing to say, I suggest you keep your idle thoughts to yourself. Now, as I was saying, it does seem a little late to start preparing for the usual class project but we do want to entertain your families and other members of the town and community around here. The Deer Lodge has offered instead to sponsor an amateur night and I thought that would be a wonderful idea."

There was a loud cheer from the class. "Hey, this sounds way better," Teddy whispered.

"But what would we do, Mrs. Beddlington?" someone asked.

"My goodness, you shouldn't have to ask me such a question, Joyce. You, for one, sing, don't you? And I know that many of you play the piano and other instruments. For example, Shirley Macrae, hiding back there, is supposed to be one of the best Highland dancers in Northern Alberta . . . and some of you could do recitations or dramatic readings . . . and I'm sure many of you have talents I've never even heard of."

They all laughed at her quip and then someone made a

motion for the amateur night program. The vote was unanimously in favor. Before dismissing the class Mrs. Beddlington asked that they all sign up within a few days so they could be assigned a number on the program.

"I shall do my acrobatic dance," Marion said as they walked home. "I can do a complete backbend and pick up my silk handkerchief from the floor with my teeth if I practice long enough . . . and maybe Mama will make me a glittering tunic to match the hankie."

"What'll we do, Sis?" little Mike said, tugging at Lisa's coat as they arrived at the front of the store. "I can't do anything except play one song on the harmonica and everyone's heard that." They waved to Marion as she departed and sat down on the front steps.

"I will sing 'I Drink to Thee Only,'" Suzanne replied. "And I'll wear Mama's black lace dress."

"Oh, I'm sure that Mama'd go for that in a big way," Teddy chuckled. "And perhaps she'll also let our diva borrow her high heels and silk stockings."

"You're just jealous 'cause you can't sing . . . 'specially now that your voice is breaking." She imitated Teddy's new voice, half high quaver, deepening into a low croak. Teddy whacked her across the back, then darted into the store before she could catch him.

Lisa knew that she could play the piano but she really didn't play very well . . . perhaps she'd write a monologue. Maybe about Florence Nightingale, walking down the hospital corridors with her lamp in her hand . . . and she'd wear a white nightgown . . . and they'd all weep. She started explaining her idea to her sister and brother.

"They might think you were Lady Macbeth instead and

that you were about to kill someone," Suzanne replied seriously. "Or that you were just plain crazy and they'd cart you away. Better think of something else."

They finally left their perch on the stoop and entered the store to attend to their various jobs. Papa pinned a list on the pantry door each morning, and they all dutifully followed it. Mike fetched a broom from the rear of the building and began scattering oily green sand on the floor to keep down the dust. Suzanne tidied the shelves and made sure the boxes were in even rows, not jutting out all over. Teddy had already dragged the heavy wagon from the warehouse. It was loaded with cans and boxes to fill the empty shelves. Lisa was stuck with the warehouse job this week and hurried to the back room to the little cubicle where she'd candle eggs. She climbed onto the stool, switched on the bare glaring light bulb, and started holding individual eggs to the light to make sure they had no dark spots.

An hour later, when she had filled several crates with the good eggs, she was still no closer to an idea for amateur night. At least their cousin might be visiting with them. Ben's parents had promised he could come to Chatko for Easter vacation so he would surely attend the concert.

"That you, Teddy?" she said as she heard the metal wheels of the wagon screech by her cubicle. Drawing back the curtain she called to him. "Teddy, I still don't have any ideas and I'd like us to be particularly good and win a prize maybe."

" 'Specially with dear cousin Ben here," he laughed. "You sort of have a crush on him, don't you, Lisa? You always talk about him and he's always writing you letters."

"Mainly about puppets," she replied. "Remember, the books he sends are for the benefit of the entire family."

"Sure, sure, he has all our interests at heart and . . . hey . . . just a moment . . . I'll be a monkey's uncle. Oh, how stupid can we get? What a bunch of fools we are." He pounded his head with his fist, meanwhile prancing all about the room.

"That's it, that's it . . . a natural."

"What on earth is wrong with you, Theodore Stein? Do tell me this very moment."

"Our puppets, Lisa, our puppets, dear stupe of a sister. That's what we'll do for amateur night. We'll put on a play."

"Oh, Teddy, to think that it never even occurred to me. How wonderful! But will they let us do a combined thing like that? Is it legal?"

"Call the others quick. Sure it's legal. As I was leaving class I distinctly heard Mrs. Beddlington tell Roddy Brown that he and his sister could sing a duet . . . so this is just a quadrangle, a quintuplet or whatever you call it. Hey Mike, Suzanne, Tom can be part of it, too . . . whoo-peeeee."

The other children came running from various corners in the store. "Hey Teddy, Papa says to hush it up and do your work," Mike cautioned.

"You sick again, Teddy?" Suzanne smirked.

"If this is being sick then it's the best sickness I ever had. I've got our entry for amateur night, kids. I have it." He told them of his plan to give a marionette production.

"How could I have forgotten them?"

"It's certain to be the best thing there."

"We'll have to make our own portable puppet theater. Have we got time to make one? It's only two weeks away."

"What will Papa say?"

"Has to be a squelch in every crowd."

"What's a squelch, Teddy?" Mike demanded.

"Somebody to spoil the fun."

Lisa shook her head and pointed out that Suzanne was correct. Papa certainly would have a fit. Particularly since he seemed to hate anything and everything about the theater. "He says that all actors come to a bad end like his sister."

"And Mama will say why did we all take lessons if we don't use them. She'll insist that we're going to make fools of ourselves and of our parents."

Teddy looked at them with a disgusted expression. Ashamed at having destroyed his enthusiasm, the three of them turned away. Things just never worked out for Teddy. Lisa moved back to her candling room, then paused.

"I have it — and it'll work; come back, everyone." Nobody had left. "We won't tell Mama and Papa. We'll tell Mama that we're going to play piano and sing and all that nonsense and then surprise her the night of the concert. She won't dare stop us when we're already onstage."

"And what are you going to do with Papa? Tie him up, I suppose."

"Don't be foolish. Remember Papa doesn't like going to the theater anyway. We'll tell him that everything is terribly amateur and he'll decide it's better to stay home. He'll never know."

It was the perfect solution and they all made plans to convince their parents of the innocence of their program. Suzanne made a practice of singing every morning before breakfast. The disgusting falsetto soprano that she used disturbed the entire house. Papa shook his head and suggested that there wasn't even a single musical member in the family. Lisa and Teddy always met at the piano after dinner while Papa attempted to have a nap under his newspaper. When Papa complained, Mama explained that it was for the show. The violin wailed as if it were feeling great pain from such a mockery of music. Lisa, who had no particular talent for the piano, found it simple to miss notes. Papa finally departed for his bedroom, mumbling that he would definitely prefer not to be a witness to their embarrassment. Finally even Mama no longer had any patience with her unmusical flock. Whenever they began making music, she shook her head in sorrow.

Meanwhile Teddy had drawn a sketch for a portable puppet theater. Tom would supervise the building. The sides and back were three huge pieces of plywood, planned so that they could be hooked together at several places so there would be no danger of their falling over. They planned to borrow two of Mama's Japanese screens to hide the sides, or wings, of the theater. This would enable them to have a place for their assorted puppets and stage properties and also would assist them in moving around freely themselves.

The theater would have to be about ten feet wide and the floor of their stage had to be high so that the entire audience might see the total production. They had already chosen and tested three huge lights from the store. They would mount these on tall poles at both front corners of the stage to make certain of adequate lighting for their theater within a theater. Since the puppets were so small they could not depend on the ordinary stage lights. Tom would make the theater in his basement. He guaranteed that it would be perfect for the big night.

The back curtain was the most important part of their theater. Not only did it have to provide a suitable background for the marionettes, but in addition it had to have the height and breadth to hide the puppeteers from their audience while they manipulated the dolls.

Suzanne had suggested cheesecloth as a cheap solution, but Lisa pointed out that cheesecloth would be transparent in the heavily lighted community hall and that the audience would see their shadows.

"We're just going to have to pool all our birthday money and buy some of that red velveteen from the store," Lisa insisted.

"Couldn't we just borrow some instead?" Suzanne suggested.

"Oh come on, Sue, cough up the money. We can't borrow material. It's not like taking leftovers. That'd be stealing."

"But I was saving for a pair of black patent shoes."

"Look, either we do this thing right or we can forget about it," Lisa said. So Suzanne dug into her bank and produced her share of the money. Lisa agreed to ask Marion to purchase the needed cloth from Mama. Mama mustn't have the slightest reason to suspect them.

"I really think Mama's getting suspicious anyway, Lisa. You know Mama's second sense. When I sang yesterday she asked me if I was practicing to be a comedian and she said that I better gargle my throat with salt or maybe forget about the amateur show altogether."

It *had* become most difficult to keep Mama in the dark. If only they could risk telling her about their theater! But of course she'd tell Papa and that would end everything. Mama absolutely never kept secrets from Papa. Even Lisa had an uneasy feeling about so many secrets. Until their move to Chatko Falls they had seldom hidden anything from Mama. And now, each day there seemed to be something new to hide. What a relief it would be when Mama finally saw the production and they brought the puppets down from the attic.

"Lisa, quit daydreaming and come help me pick the puppets for the show. I thought we'd start by having a circus parade. What do you think?"

Lisa liked the idea. Their Big Top group offered a dramatic opening and an excuse to use animals and characters from several plays. There were two aerialists in sleek tights; a clown dressed in polka dots had a sad face and a strawberry nose. The lion tamer in his red jacket and black-painted boots even had two lions cut from an old mop. Then there was the patchwork-quilt elephant and some zingy acrobats. It would be a perfect opening to put the audience in a relaxed mood.

After taking a vote on which play to perform they had finally decided on *Sleeping Beauty* because it was familiar. There was a princess with lovely wavy blond hair made from thick silk cord they had unwound; the bad fairy looked a fright with her long hooked nose, piercing eyes and flowing black cape.

They had even made a twinkling blue castle with huge turrets fashioned from cardboard and cellophane. This was for the big scene where the prince breaks through the enchanted forest.

Tom had gathered loads of evergreen boughs for the fierce hedge. There was even a tiny spinning wheel for the heroine to prick her finger on. Lisa was rather disappointed that they hadn't chosen one of her plays to perform, but she agreed that if the audience had trouble hearing over the noise, they still would understand the motions in a familiar fairy story.

"Suzanne, you'll be property mistress . . . that means you have to keep a close eye on all the dolls," Teddy commanded. "Remember we'll all have to work more than one doll, and of course when there is the huge court christening scene and the one where they're all sleeping, we'll prop up several dolls on chairs or stools in the ballroom."

"And maybe we'll win the big prize," Tom added.

"What prize?"

"Didn't you see it on the bulletin board at school today? Gee, there was a huge crowd around it."

"Come on, Tom, get to the point."

"Well, the Deer have decided to give prizes to the best people. Three prizes . . . and the big one is twenty dollars and a chance to perform at some theater night in Edmonton. What do you think of that?"

What did they think? It was wonderful. What luck, what an opportunity. To be able to perform in a big city in front of a real audience.

"I meant the money, silly."

"Oh, the money, sure it'll come in handy to buy material for a really good puppet theater. But to be onstage in a real theater like . . ."

"Like Mr. Majunko."

"Why, then we'd be genuine actors, wouldn't we?"

They were all elated. Now they really had to win. There was no longer any question. Then they began discussing their competition.

"Don't be so sure. Don't count your chickens before they hatch, as Mama always says," Suzanne answered. "Why, the

Macrae girl already has some trophies for doing the sword dance at the Highland Games, and Bobby Small is practically a professional on the ukulele.''

"And some of those acrobats are fantastic and you should see Marion's costume, with spangles.''

There was no use worrying about their competition. "Papa always says to do your best at anything, and if you've tried your hardest, then you can't do anything more. At least then you can be proud of your efforts.'' Lisa paused. There was an eerie silence. Lisa had chosen a bad time to mention Papa because, despite their brave talk, they all secretly shared the same hidden fear that tormented her. What if Papa came to the concert after all? What then?

10

Keeping Secrets

THE WICKED FAIRY HAS DISAPPEARED. Who took her? Where is that witch? Lisa, did you pack the witch separately from the other puppets? Bring her here right away."

"And what's wrong with you, Teddy? I never had the witch at all. She must be in the big picnic hamper with all the other puppets . . . unless you took her to the community hall already?"

"Mike, did you take the witch — you know, the bad fairy for the play . . . she's missing."

"Never saw no witch since yesterday. 'Oh, once there was a wicked, wicked witch . . . there was, there was. And she was the fiercest, meanest witch . . . because, because.'" Mike hummed the song of the witch, ducking as Teddy tried to grab his arm.

"Stop singing that silly song this moment, Mike. Don't you realize that if we can't find the witch, our play will be ruined? The concert starts in just about an hour! It's no joke; she really has disappeared. We've got everything set up over there and practically all the puppets are at the hall, but no bad fairy." Teddy thumped his hand on the dining room table to emphasize his remarks.

Lisa and Mike both shook their heads. Nothing must happen at this late hour to spoil their production. There had been so many problems to cope with already.

First, they had been forced to take Mrs. Beddlington into their confidence. There had been no way to hide their need to appear as a combined number in the amateur show. She had really been most surprised.

"Oh, hand puppets," she said. "How sweet. I used to play with them when I was a child."

Teddy had been insulted by her remark and growled back that they were not hand puppets but professional marionettes. Then, after they had sworn her to secrecy, she refused to believe that their parents knew nothing about the dolls.

"You couldn't possibly construct puppets all these months without your parents finding out about it."

"But we have our own special, private place in the attic and Papa would be furious if he knew . . . so please, please just list us on the program as a surprise group."

"Don't you children live at home with your parents, or are they away all the time?" Mrs. Beddlington had continued, making it sound as if their parents were either ignorant or not interested in their children.

Teddy immediately explained that they certainly did live with their parents, and that, although both senior Steins worked in the store, they all lived right above it; Lisa added that their parents were wonderful, helpful parents but that Papa hated the theater. When they tried to explain this, you'd have thought they were some sort of sideshow freaks. Finally they brought a sample puppet for her to see, but she still couldn't understand their problem.

It had taken another long explanation from Lisa to make the teacher agree to keep their secret. She only made the promise when they insisted they would withdraw from the show entirely if she told Papa.

"You see, he's from Europe," Lisa said, as if this explained anything. "And he doesn't think we should waste our time on . . . on frivolous things." She had concluded with the perfect expression, or at least this explanation seemed to satisfy Mrs. Beddlington.

Perhaps it was because she was distracted by other children waiting to see her about accompanists for their songs or staging or other problems, but eventually Mrs. Beddlington allowed them to prepare for their performance without listing it as a marionette theater. As they were leaving she murmured something about "having a talk with your mother after the show," but that was fine. By then it would be too late for Mama to do anything. She'd lecture them, but Mama's lectures weren't hard to take.

There'd been so many little problems, and now they had a missing puppet. Here they were, all prepared to leave the house, hoping to escape before Papa came up from the store, and the most important doll in the play was missing.

"Hey, what's wrong with all of you? I shouldn't think you'd be glum on a night like this." It was Ben. He'd arrived just a few hours ago from Edmonton. Lisa couldn't help smiling when he entered the room. She was so pleased to have him here. Poor Ben, there'd been so many last-minute chores before the show that she'd been too busy to spend very much time with him so far. Suzanne had given him a tour of the store since Lisa and Teddy were dashing all over the place. Too bad she wouldn't be able to sit with him very long at the concert. He'd have to sit with Mama. Ben had grown so tall since her visit to Edmonton. He was really very handsome, with his fair, straight hair and laughing eyes.

"Our most important puppet is missing, Ben. We can't put on a performance without her."

Then all three Stein children turned to look at Suzanne, who had entered behind Ben. Suzanne was momentarily on a different planet, blinking her long eyelashes at Ben, and patting her curls. She was doing her best to impress this charming city cousin.

"Duchess Stein, could you please join our simple world long enough to think about the missing puppet? Didn't you take her to your room yesterday to fit on her wings?" Teddy asked.

Suzanne stuck out her tongue at Teddy from behind Ben's back. Then she paused and her mouth formed a huge O. Wailing, she rushed toward her room. Nobody moved so much as an inch until she returned.

"I, I left it on my bed . . . was going to put it up in the attic before school this morning and . . . and I forgot. Oh, Teddy, she's not there now. Nowhere."

They were all too shocked to bawl her out. It was totally nauseating. Obviously Suzanne was mortified by her mistake for she was snuffling in her hanky and not batting her eyes at all now.

"What on earth is going on here and why aren't all of you dressed up for the concert?" Mama stood facing them.

"Suzanne, have you got a stomachache? Lisa, why don't

you wear your pretty dress? You planned on playing the piano in those old clothes? And Teddy, your hair is standing up all over the place. What kind of children have I raised? Your cousin comes here 'specially to visit with you and you're too busy to be with him. And now you look like a bunch of tramps.''

They had forgotten. Naturally Mama didn't know that they'd get filthy, working the props behind the stage. And why wear good clothes when no one would see them anyway? But this was a bad slip-up.

"Oh, we're just about to get dressed now, Mama. Leaving it to the last minute as usual."

"Mama, Mama, maybe you saw a strange old-looking pup . . . doll, that is, sitting on my bed this morning?" Suzanne asked.

"Why yes, I did but I thought it was so ugly and shabby looking that I had Lucy throw it in the junk box behind the stairs, but . . ."

Suzanne didn't wait for her to conclude. Like a cat after a bird she sprang across the room toward the stairs. Mike turned to streak after her but Teddy grabbed his arm immediately and held it tightly.

A momentary frown warned the others that Mama's suspicions would surface if they were foolish enough to show their concern. Mama shrugged as they waited for Suzanne's return. Sure enough, she carried the wicked fairy, slightly rumpled but otherwise fine. Tom hurried forward to receive the puppet from Suzanne and paused as Mr. Stein met him at the top of the stairwell. Then Tom hurtled down the steps two at a time, the puppet tucked under his arm, before Papa could speak. Their father shook his head and gave Lisa and Teddy a piercing stare.

Papa complained about their strange friends who dashed in and out like hooligans. He also wanted to know why there was such a commotion over a doll. "Thought you'd all outgrown dolls by now. And since when have dolls become one of your hobbies, Teddy?"

"It belongs to one of our friends. Suzanne borrowed it to make a new costume for it."

Papa didn't appear to believe them. "Are you four up to some monkey business again? I won't have any of that. You know, Ben, this family of mine always seems to be doing something strange. I closed the store early tonight. Seems like everybody in the entire district is going to the show at the hall and just maybe, maybe I'll come and see how my own amateurs do." He smiled at them and pinched Mike's cheek.

"Why, isn't that nice, Uncle," said Ben, who knew perfectly well that it was terrible.

Lisa managed a weak, watery smile, Mike simply gurgled through his teeth and Teddy stood looking aghast.

"But you think amateurs are a bore, Papa. You'd hate it." Suzanne nodded beside Teddy.

Mama glared at them, her lips pursed in a disappointed expression. Here was Papa finally willing to join in their plans, and now none of them were welcoming him.

Casually Teddy moved over to pick up his violin case. Gee, he'd almost forgotten that he was to take it with him and then ditch it in the cloakroom. Lisa hoped that Teddy would keep his mouth shut. If he dared to say another word to Papa then for sure Papa'd insist on coming or else he'd know something was wrong. Papa was like a mule that way.

"You know, your Papa once worked backstage himself when he was a young man. Don't make faces at me like that,

Irving," she said to Papa. "Of course he forgot about it
after that business with his sister Ida; he got the theater out
of his blood and went on to try many other things . . . but
he certainly knows about the stage, so don't ever think
otherwise."

"Didn't know that, Mama," Suzanne mumbled. The
others expressed their surprise.

"Oh, we'd love to have you come with us, Uncle," Ben
said. "My dad's always too busy for such things. It's nice to
know that you have time." Nobody made a comment.

Teddy opened the fiddle case even though it was getting
late. He rubbed his fingers on the bow as if he really loved
the old violin. Yesterday, in the middle of practicing, he
had thrown the bow halfway across the room. Now he
raised the instrument to his chin. "Think I'll practice just
once more," he said, as he tuned it. "Doing the Brahms, the
one you love, Papa."

Oh, how idiotic, Lisa thought. Now Papa would be sure
to come.

And then it happened. An unbelievably weird and wild
sound came from the instrument. Teddy hit so many flat
notes that even Mama cringed. But Teddy appeared to be
in raptures as he swayed back and forth.

"Ah, I think I finally have it . . . the melody is coming." He looked like a dying man as he pressed the violin
closer to his chin. His eyes closed as he rocked back on his
heels. The violin wailed as if this insult demanded a reply.
The tone could only be compared to the sound of a trapped
animal and grew louder each moment as Teddy carefully
ripped the Brahms to shreds.

"Enough already . . . enough . . . and we are supposed to pay good money to hear that? Ha, my poor

Brahms. . . . Maybe in ten more years you'll manage to stop destroying him," Papa cried, waving the violin aside.

Teddy finally lowered the instrument and gave Papa a wide-eyed stare. "So I'm not yet a Menuhin, but the tone is coming."

"Only piece of wood you should handle is a hockey stick. I hope that some of the others are more talented than you." He glared at all of them and apologized to Ben. Mama reminded them that it was time to leave so they hurriedly changed their clothes, still unsure whether Teddy's act had succeeded.

When they returned to the kitchen Mama was taking a steaming bowl out of the oven. It was fish for Papa, who hadn't yet had his dinner. "Now you look like humans. Even if you're not so talented you should at least make me proud that you're well-groomed."

There was a long ring from the telephone. Suzanne called Papa. They couldn't tell whether this call was local because Papa always shouted into the receiver. The conversation was a long one and Papa continued to talk, explaining with his hands, to make certain the caller understood him. Finally he moved back from the mouthpiece on the wall phone and put the receiver back on the hook.

"Jake Mueller. Needs some supplies and his old truck finally gave up. All his neighbors already have gone into town for this darn concert. Only a few miles out. Said I'd bring the things out to him. Sorry, but it looks like I'll have to miss your performances, children. Too bad, but Mueller's a good customer, and he's got a big family out there."

Completely unaware of their relief, Papa continued to apologize. Lisa had to kick Mike in the shins for he'd been ready to give a whoop of delight.

"We'll miss you, Papa."

"Too bad, Papa, perhaps you'll be able to come another time."

"Oh, Irving, what a disappointment . . . and the children will miss you. No other general store owner gives his customers such service. You're working too hard." Mama really seemed unhappy. Perhaps she felt she needed someone to lean on when her children gave their miserable performances. They grabbed their coats, and winking at each other, prepared to leave the house.

"Better drive slowly on the roads, Papa. They're usually very slippery and dangerous this time of the year. Take it slow and easy, don't rush."

Papa looked questioningly at Teddy. "What brought on this sudden concern? I've always managed to drive without your advice up until now."

"Why, Irving, Irving, your children just love you. Don't always be suspicious. We're all concerned that you should take care of yourself."

They kissed Papa good-bye in front of the store, not moving toward the community hall until they saw the last glimmer of his car as he headed south toward the Mueller farm.

Then each of the children quietly congratulated Teddy on his masterful performance before their parents. Even if it hadn't done the trick, they were certain it had assisted Papa in making his decision to forsake the school show.

I I

The Curtain Goes Up

THE COMMUNITY HALL had never held such a huge crowd. Every single chair in the place was occupied and the janitor, with the assistance of some students, was hauling up wooden benches from the basement to make room for the people who were still flooding through the door.

"My gosh, there are more people here than at the flower show or the giant Bingo. Never knew there were so many people in the district."

"Can you imagine it, there are folks here from as far away as Hillbury?"

"Where on earth will we sit?" Mama asked in dismay. Lisa put one arm around Mama and hesitantly reached for Ben's outstretched hand with her other arm as she led them toward the front of the room. Tom had reserved seats for the entire family in the second row. Mama was pleased, and didn't even notice that there had been no place saved for their father. Lisa and Teddy sat down but found it difficult to concentrate on any conversation. Finally the lights dimmed and the curtain descended on the stage.

"What a strange curtain," Ben remarked. It really was different from the usual velvet stage curtain. The curtain was canvas and looked like a patchwork quilt with a mass of colored squares. Instead of dividing in the middle, the curtain rolled upwards like a store awning. Each huge square advertised some type of store or product. The curtain must have been very old, for some of the products listed didn't even exist in Chatko any longer.

There was the Gaylord Blacksmith Shoppe; Mackie's Shoe Repairs, which featured a giant high-heeled boot; Dr. Robinson's Rebirth Potion, which naturally displayed a medicine bottle, and a host of other colorful ads. In the center of the curtain was an enormous buffalo head with a huge staring eye. Lisa told Ben about the hole in the animal's eye. Using this secret peephole, the performers could peer unseen at their audience before a program began.

"Do you have to go now?" Ben whispered as they sat down at the conclusion of singing "God Save the King."

Lisa shook her head. "We're in the second half of the show. Don't have to leave until after intermission." She still couldn't believe that Ben was sitting here beside her. In the past number of months she had exchanged so many letters with him, but now that he was next to her she found it difficult to open her mouth.

Now the benches were also packed as heavily clad citizens entered from the still wintry street. Fathers herded their children in Hudson's Bay blanket coats, white with wide green and red stripes; brown woolen stockings bulged over their ankle-length combination underwear.

Toddlers sat patiently as their mothers unbuckled galoshes from their feet and tugged off bulky leggings. The pool hall owner proudly escorted his two costumed daughters. Their flower petal hats with crepe paper stems made them look like some strange variety of insect.

A pale young violinist with greased-down bangs was supported by his parents, each clutching one of his elbows. Every parent whispered advice to his particular prodigy while the crackling of paper sacks containing home-made fudge and popcorn balls added to the din.

Several girls from school walked down the aisles distributing ballots and programs to the audience. The mayor, a pudgy man, appeared on the stage to welcome them. He told the audience that they were privileged to have a panel of judges from the city . . . an actor, a school inspector and an alderman. There was a round of applause for the judges when they acknowledged the introduction.

"However, these ballots are for you. There will also be a prize for the most popular act . . . perhaps one that does not have the professional merit to be the judges' choice but one that appeals to you, the community.

"A special thanks to Mrs. Beddlington who has been so co-operative in organizing the show with me. And now without further ado . . . I give you the Chatko Falls Follies."

Lisa glanced down the list of names on the yellow program Ben handed her. There they were, number twenty-five on the program. It merely listed their names and called them a "Combined Performance."

"Liseleh, they've made some mistake. Go call the mayor. They have all of you listed together. Oh dear." Mama peered more closely at the program through her glasses.

"Must just be a typographical error, Mama. No need to disturb the mayor," Suzanne quickly replied.

Fortunately the curtain was rolled up once again before Mama was able to call the mayor. The first act was a juggler, but he lost most of his rubber balls on the stage and one of his Indian clubs sailed down to the audience. Giggles of laughter followed.

This performance was followed by the Perkins twins reciting "My Shadow." "I have a little shadow that goes in and out with me," the number one twin droned, gesturing with a rigid arm toward number two standing slightly behind him.

The lesser shadow sidestepped to avoid being hit in the face by his identically dressed brother. The mutual wigwagging motions continued. Number two shot up "like an india rubber ball" on cue and then curled up a "sleepyhead" as they mumbled the conclusion. Then, counting to three out loud, they bowed and left the stage.

Then some girl in lemon velvet shorts did a tap dance standing on her head. A small elevated platform served as her upside-down stage.

"Never saw anything like that before," Mama said. "Poor little girl will get a headache." Ben was bent over double laughing. At first Lisa wanted to join him, but immediately she had visions of him laughing in the same way at their coming performance.

Next there were four boys in aprons who called themselves a barbershop quartet. The only problem was that the smallest boy drowned out the voices of the others. But the audience warmed to the performers, and as the appreciation increased the clapping was less sporadic and more enthusiastic.

There were several sopranos, all carrying long hankies, on the program, and Ben asked if they had colds or something. The poor Finch boy gave a thunderous version of "The Charge of the Light Brigade" and then forgot the final stanza. He stood there mute until Mrs. Beddlington's voice could be heard loud and clear prompting him from the wings.

At this point Lisa got the shivers. She pulled her coat more tightly around her shoulders but still she shook. She was unable to hear the dancers and instrumentalists that followed. She was petrified. What if they forgot their lines? Who would help them? Oh, it had all been a big mistake. There was still time to have Mrs. Beddlington scratch them from the program. Nobody knew what they were doing anyway. She turned to Teddy but he was watching the stage. Ben seemed to understand her fears for he awkwardly patted her shoulder and winked. Mike was making horrible faces at her from the other side of Mama, motions that suggested he was about to be sick. However, when Mama looked down at him he straightened his shoulders and gave her an innocent smile.

"Oh, isn't Marion gorgeous? Look at her, Lisa," Suzanne whispered. Marion wore an unbelievable pair of spangled green tights with a sparkling bodice. She also had green stockings and green ribbons in her hair. She cart-wheeled her way across the stage and then stopped long enough to go into a great spin, like a top. The audience gasped when she completed a series of handstands by flipping right over in the air. Absolutely weightless. For her finale she did a full backbend. With great suppleness she bent backwards and reached for a green silk scarf placed on the floor. She picked it up with her teeth, then flipped up on her feet with the piece of silk still intact in her mouth. There was a great gasp. Marion bent forward in a curtsy and then raised her arms to the audience, as Lisa had suggested. The boys in the audience whistled and clapped wildly.

"Oh, there's just no use trying now, Teddy. She'll win it . . . she's a shoo-in," Suzanne said.

"Boy, that girl sure is talented, and what looks," Ben replied. Lisa felt a pang of envy. If only Ben would use that tone of voice in speaking of her! For a moment she regretted that she wasn't doing something solo so she might at least look attractive. She crouched down in her seat. Perhaps Mrs. Beddlington had forgotten them. As the audience stretched during the intermission she called to Teddy to suggest they forget the whole thing.

"Ah, there you are, Steins. Backstage immediately. Quietly now. Through the side door there. Really, did you forget? I said that as soon as the curtain falls, second act performers backstage. Anyone see Jerry Bashford? I can't find him either. Hurry, everyone, hurry."

Mrs. Beddlington had grasped Lisa's arm before she could even blow Mama a kiss. She was steered with the boys and Suzanne through the stage door while Ben whispered good luck to their backs. They fumbled their way down the narrow cement steps to the dressing rooms below the stage. There were two dressing rooms upstairs, but it was far too cramped for all the performers to gather there.

What bedlam backstage! Not at all like the professional theater she had seen in the city. A fat girl was having trouble doing up the zipper of her fluffy organdy dress and called to Lisa for assistance. Mrs. Macrae stood applying bright red lipstick to Shirley's lips.

"Shirley, purse your lips tightly, that's better . . . no,

no, don't smirk. Is your kilt pin straight? Never mind those other children. This is your show. Just concentrate on winning."

Shirley picked up her gilt-coated swords, fitted her velvet tam on her head, and tossed her short yellow curls at Suzanne. Lisa thought the curls looked like wood shavings, glued to her head. What a nasty girl.

"Gee, I wish I could be seen in a lovely dress instead of scrunching up behind our stage in the dust," Suzanne said longingly.

Lisa shrugged her shoulders as she searched for Teddy and Tom. Finally she found Teddy at the very back of the basement. He motioned for her to join him backstage.

"Just enough time to check our theater before the next act goes on. Come on Lisa, stop shaking. We're the best and you've all got to believe that."

It was dark on the stage now and Lisa tripped as she followed him. Picking herself up from the grimy floor, she wiped her hands. The stage had a second set of curtains near the back and the puppet theater stood behind them. Lisa checked the puppets with Teddy, pausing to fondle a favorite before she returned to the dressing rooms.

"Oh, bring us luck," she whispered, giving the doll a kiss.

"Number twenty please, onstage now. Number twenty-one follow. Will the next four numbers line up here in the wings . . . now, now."

Mrs. Beddlington seemed to be everywhere at once. "Now don't forget your numbers. Yoohoo, Miss Jones, you are to accompany the following two performers, so check your music and for goodness sakes remember that Larry has 'Danny Boy' and the Kantowitz girl needs the Ukrainian melody for her dance. Remember, you forgot during rehearsals."

Again the house lights dimmed as the curtain began to creak its way up. Larry Harrigan had a mellow tenor voice and his "Danny Boy" was wonderful.

"He'll win, for sure he'll win."

Lisa turned to speak to the girl behind her. The girl had her hand clapped over her mouth. "Oh, I can't go on . . . quick someone give me a towel, I'm going to be . . ." The girl rushed toward the dressing room, pushing past the row of waiting children.

While Mrs. Beddlington announced that number twenty-two would be unable to perform, Lisa grabbed Suzanne's hand. "Now look straight ahead," she hissed, surprised at the note of command in her voice. "That won't happen to you. You have a cast-iron stomach, Mama says." Suzanne nodded, but her face was drained of all color.

"Oh dear, the poor Hindley child. Anyone have some aspirin?" Mrs. Beddlington asked.

Shirley Macrae pranced onto the stage, and as the footlights were turned up, she began her precise sword dance. Such confidence. And her nose was raised so high. Perfectly executed.

"Just look at that turned-up nose," Suzanne whispered.

And then as she was completing an intricate step across her sword, Shirley's dainty black slipper misbehaved. Her hopes, along with the golden sword, went flinging wildly across the stage. A great gasp from the audience. Shirley stopped moving; the pianist, hidden in the corner, blithely continued to play the Scottish tune. The children in the wings gazed at Shirley in alarm.

"Oh, shut up, you fool," Shirley shrieked at the accompanist as she retrieved her swords. Hysterical giggles from below appeared to enrage her further and, grabbing her swords, she stamped off the stage.

"How awful, not to complete her dance. Whatever you do, finish the play, no matter how many goofs you make. Don't ever insult an audience. The show must go on," Teddy told them.

Lisa was certain that number twenty-four had just gone on, but Mrs. Beddlington was pushing them toward the stage.

"Number twenty-five. Do hurry. I told them to hold the curtain longer this time to give you a chance to move your theater forward. Good luck, children."

Then they were alone on the empty stage, pushing the theater carefully toward the closed curtain. It took their combined strength to move the heavy puppet theater and it swayed with each step.

"Oh, it won't work, Teddy. It's going to fall over."

"Nothing I build ever falls," Tom said.

"My throat's all closed up. I can't talk."

"Did you remember to tell Mrs. Beddlington to start the Circus Parade song as soon as the curtain begins to go up?" Lisa asked Teddy. Teddy nodded and then turned his warm smile on all of them, as if this was just a performance in the attic. Now Lisa was relieved that their faces would be hidden behind the curtains. At least with puppets, the audience didn't see you. You could almost pretend that you weren't really there . . . like an invisible person.

"Quick, Lisa, take a peek through the eye."

"You do it, Teddy."

"Got too many butterflies."

Lisa tiptoed to the vacant eye of the buffalo, and peered

through it. What a mass of cabbage heads the audience seemed, all staring intently at the curtain. She couldn't even see Mama. She heard the creak of the curtain as it began to rise and rushed back to her position behind the theater.

"Think of them as cabbage heads, just rows and rows of cabbages," she whispered to the other four children. "That's all they are." Suzanne's hunched shoulders dropped and Teddy even managed a smile. Perhaps this would help them.

The sudden glare of the lights focusing on them from all directions caused them to blink. Then the music began.

"Hurry, hurry, hurry, ladies and gentlemen . . . get your tickets now before it's too late — for the Greatest Show on Earth. The Big Top," shouted the lion tamer, swishing his whip as he crossed the stage.

The acrobats somersaulted across the stage with Mike's dilapidated lions rolling behind. The clown plopped down on the stage while the trapeze artists gestured to the audience. "And now, ladies and genemumms, we present the Bigtop Buskins in a heart-stirring performance of *The Sleeping Beauty*," Teddy announced from behind the curtain as the ringmaster again cracked his whip.

There had been a sudden lull as the audience realized that they were seeing a puppet performance. Now as the circus performers bowed and turned to the stage, there were oh's and ah's but no applause. Oh dear, were the people sitting on their hands? Obviously they didn't care for marionettes. Lisa ducked down, reaching for the good fairy. The wicked fairy flew about the stage, her wings flapping violently as Teddy snarled at the stricken king and queen. What a hideous laugh that was! Then it was

Lisa's cue to make her pronouncement of the long sleep for all the members of the court, the spell which would finally be broken by the kiss of the brave prince.

By the time the prince had climbed the enchanted hedge and kissed Sleeping Beauty, lying on her lovely canopied bed, Lisa sensed that this was the best performance they had ever given.

"But no one's clapped at all. It's so silent out there," Teddy whispered.

"Maybe everyone's gone home, including your city cousin," Tom replied as Lisa's godmother swooped down to bless the happy bride and groom. At this point they were all far too occupied to converse since they had to manipulate the many dolls of the court as they awoke from their hundred-year sleep. All the members of the cast bowed or curtsied to the audience. The velveteen curtain was finally closed and they all sighed with relief.

"Now they'll all clap," Suzanne gasped. But there was silence. A long painful silence. Mike already had tears in his eyes.

"More, we want more," someone shouted. And suddenly there were great gusts of applause. And stamping and shouting and whistling. The thunder of the response seemed to fill the hall. The five children stood grinning at each other. Then they drew together in a spontaneous embrace.

"I guess they liked us after all," Teddy said as they waited for the big curtain to fall. When it dropped they raced off to the wings. Still more clapping and the curtain creaked upwards again. The five of them stood smiling in the wings.

"Don't be dummies," Mrs. Beddlington said. "Go onstage. They want to see you. That was excellent, just perfect."

She pushed them out onto the stage. Lost without their protective covering, the five of them hesitantly walked toward the center of the stage, arms linked. Eyes downward, they bowed very low. Another burst of applause and they ran off the stage.

Lisa wasn't even aware of the acts that followed them. All that mattered was that the people had liked their puppets, really thought that they were good. When the final performer left the stage many of the participants returned to their seats as the judges headed for the stage. The Steins conferred and decided they'd better wait backstage until it was over. Maybe Mama would go ahead home.

"Come on now, children. Everyone back to their seats. What are you skulking back here for? Shoo. Out with you." Mrs. Beddlington pushed them through the door.

"Do you think we have a chance at a prize?" Mike asked.

"Maybe, maybe, but Marion was so good and did you see the way everyone looked at that violin player?" They searched for Mama and hastened toward her. Mama had tears in her eyes and did not appear to be angry.

"My babies, how wonderful. When did you do it? Why didn't you tell me? I was so proud of all of you." Mama kissed each of them, including Tom, as they settled into their chairs.

"Gee, that was absolutely the greatest," Ben said, and kissed Lisa on her cheek. Blushing, Lisa looked up to see Tom frowning in the distance. Didn't Tom like Ben? The curtain was up again as the judges, the mayor and Mrs. Beddlington walked across the stage to chairs behind a long table.

"It has been so difficult to make a decision today . . . you were all so very good," one of the judges began. In the distance there was a low murmuring, followed by an audible muttering as some commotion at the back of the hall increased in volume.

The judge raised his voice to be heard above the noise coming from the rear. Still the racket persisted. "And so we will start with the number three selection first. To that most skilled dancer, Miss Marion . . ." his voice was drowned out as the disturbance drew closer to them. It was obvious that someone was pushing violently through the crowd. "How dare you elbow me like that?"

"You shoved my wife."

"Please lower your voices, friends," called the mayor.

Lisa gave Suzanne a squeeze as the clapping muffled the competitive sound. "Gee, I'm so happy for Marion. I think she should have been first, she was so . . ."

"Honest with her parents," a foghorn barked in her ear. "Not like some children I know. Pretending they were playing instruments, telling lies. Nothing but falsehoods."

And then the source of the turmoil reached them as Papa, looking deranged, loomed in back of them. His face was an over-ripe tomato as he raged at them.

"Aha, take your time, Papa, don't rush back from the farm. Wanted me to miss it, eh? When did you make those fantastic puppets, when you were supposed to be studying for exams? Doing your chores? Well, answer me, why don't you?" His bald head was covered with beads of perspiration and his hands shook as he spoke.

Mama tried to shush Papa, to make him lower his voice. It was useless. Dimly, in the distant world, Lisa heard the judge talking. "And to that very talented tenor, the singer of 'Danny Boy,' the second prize. Come up here, young Mr. Harrigan, and receive your justly deserved award."

There was applause and a few cheers. Someone demanded that Papa sit down and stop blocking the view. Papa reached for Mike's arm and lifted him from his chair.

"Home, right now you will come home. Telling lies to your father, making a fool of me."

"Please, Irving, let them wait until it is over, only a few more minutes and then you can punish them," Mama pleaded in vain. Even Teddy was too shocked at Papa's unexpected appearance to risk speaking back.

"*Now,* this very instant we go home." Papa pulled them down the aisle with Mama and Ben bringing up the rear. Even Tom seemed to feel that he had to obey Papa's wishes.

It was difficult to break through the audience to reach the rear doors of the hall. Many people were standing up against the walls to have a better view of the judges. People whispered words of praise, clapped them on their shoulders and tried to shake their hands as they marched meekly down the side aisle. Papa was going to make them the laughingstock of the school in addition to punishing them.

"And now for our grand winner," the judge said. "Without a doubt this was the most talented, original act we have seen in some years. This was brilliant theater. There were many fine performances tonight but all the judges concurred on this one. Yes, friends, this one really deserved to win. It had that star quality. So without any further ado I will call upon that brilliant Stein family and their partner Tom to come forward and accept first prize for their magical puppet theater! Congratulations and we'll look forward to seeing more of this family when they tread the boards again. A fine young group of thespians."

They were almost at the door when they halted to hear the judge. Mama and Papa had also stopped. Despite Papa, the five of them threw their arms around each other. Ben was jumping in the air with them. Oh, they had won even if Papa wouldn't let them receive their prize. They had *won* it.

"We made it."

"We won. We did it, we won the prize."

"Irving," Mama's tone was harsh. "Let them get the prize. So maybe they were wrong but you must let them receive their prize."

Papa paused and sucked in his cheeks. "Go," he said pointing to the stage. "Go up there. We won't insult this town. Get your prize but come back immediately. Then I'll decide what to do with you."

Teddy turned recklessly from his father and dashed toward the stage as if a hive of wasps were after him. "He is a tyrant," Teddy stormed to no one in particular, "but he's not going to break me or tame me." The applause was deafening and Lisa barely heard Teddy as he continued to seethe.

Lisa didn't think she had ever felt so many different sensations at the same time. Tears streamed down her cheeks. It was a strange feeling, since she never cried. Friends hugged them as they pushed their way back through the mob to the stage. Teddy was way ahead of them now and had stopped shaking his head in a violent manner. Tom cleared a space for her and Mike to slip through while Suzanne skipped behind them.

As they climbed the steps to the stage the tears continued to dribble down her cheeks. They shook hands with the officials and received a broad grin from Mrs. Beddlington. The stamping from the crowd made it impossible to think clearly. Lisa wondered briefly if her tears came from delight at having won the grand award or from shame at having deceived Papa.

12

Judgment Day

THERE WAS NO CELEBRATION in the Stein home the following morning, despite their victory in the Follies. Papa had marched them home immediately after their platform appearance. Teddy clutched the giant silver loving cup that was part of the first-prize winnings. Glaring at the trophy, Papa herded them like a flock of sheep, down the main street toward the store.

They had planned to go to the Club Café for chocolate sundaes after the concert, but no one dared mention this to Papa.

"To bed immediately. I am so angry now that I wouldn't trust myself to talk to you," he had said.

However, that hadn't prevented him from punishing them. Each of them had received four whacks on outstretched palms with Papa's thick leather belt.

"I hate doing this but it's for your own good," Papa said. "There will be no liars in this home."

Lisa's eyes were moist as she received her punishment, but they were tears of humiliation. Suzanne, whimpering all the time, managed to drop her hands slightly each time the strap fell. There was no submission on Teddy's part as he walked directly to his father.

"Hit me if it makes you feel good. It'll be your last chance," he muttered between his teeth as he stared coldly at Papa.

The strap really stung but as Mike said, wiping away his tears, "Way better than the years when we used to get it across the behind. Guess it means we've grown up."

Ben had been thoughtful enough to disappear with Tom as soon as they reached the store. If he had attended their punishment Lisa certainly would have run away from home herself. Tom had been prepared to share in their punishment but Papa had sent him away. Tom suggested that Ben join him for a walk, although they certainly hadn't been companions earlier in the evening.

The phone kept ringing while they choked on their breakfast the following morning. Several of the calls were for Lisa, but Papa refused to allow her to answer the phone even when it was Mrs. Beddlington.

"Let them congratulate her some other time."

The phone kept ringing throughout the meal. Who could swallow eggs on a day like this? Lisa pushed the fried eggs around her plate and watched them gradually shrivel up until the plump yellow centers were hollowed out like craters.

"Children, eat up or you'll get sick," Mama urged. Trying to stimulate a conversation, Ben talked about his high school. This only brought forth an occasional nod, for all they could think of was their future punishment.

"Finish quick and go into the parlor. Wasting good food when the poor people of the world are starving."

"Then you give it to the poor people, Papa. I think they need it more than we do today," Mike replied, pushing his plate toward his father.

Mike had intended no joke but Papa was insulted. "No smart cracks from you, whippersnapper."

For the first time that Lisa remembered, Mama quickly removed the plates. Perhaps she realized that any discussion of food would only prolong the tension.

"What do you think he'll really do to us?"

"He already strapped us so maybe it's another lecture."

"What if he makes us return the cup and the prize money?"

"Could be worse. What if he takes the puppets away instead?"

"Shhhh, don't even think such a terrible thing."

"You know he's even mad enough to destroy them."

They stood whispering in the living room waiting for Papa, who was taking another phone message.

"If he does anything to our puppets I'll run away from home," Teddy announced. "Why they're just like my family, not just wooden people."

"I don't think Papa plans on anything that drastic," Lisa replied with uncertainty.

Ben offered to sneak the puppets out of the house. He suggested that they hide them at Tom's. All four of the Stein children just shook their heads. Tom had arrived at the back door during breakfast but Papa had refused him entrance. Lisa felt she must give Ben some explanation. Stammering, she attempted to explain that if Papa had made up his mind to get rid of the puppets, he'd scour the entire town to find them. Naturally he'd check at Tom's home first.

"My gosh, you make your father sound like a bloodhound or some terrible monster," Ben chided, trying to make them smile.

"Well, isn't he?" Teddy replied coldly.

Lisa put a restraining hand on Teddy's shoulder. Poor Ben, here he'd come all the way from the city for a happy vacation and instead of being entertained he'd become involved in their problems with Papa. Obviously Ben would never return, nor would they be welcome in Edmonton. Just wait until he told his parents about the crazy Steins. Well, when this whole nasty experience was concluded, Lisa wanted to disappear forever. She imagined her city cousins giggling about the insane family in Chatko Falls. And most of all about their wild father.

Just then Papa entered the room, buttoning his vest as he walked toward them. Ben disappeared through the door. Papa marched around them trying to read their minds with his piercing gray eyes. Then he paced back and forth, his fingers constantly buttoning and unbuttoning the vest. He seemed disturbed and when he finally spoke his accent appeared heavier than usual.

"What did I ever do to deserve this? Am I Ghengis Khan or Rasputin?"

There was no reply since none of them knew who either of these men were. They stared at him blankly.

"Aha, so you do think I am some sort of mad dictator? That's what you think of your father, is it? And here I always thought that I was doing the best for you. Music lessons, books, trips all around the entire continent."

His gray eyes were mournful now. Someone had to reply, Lisa thought, and she turned to the others. They all stared at the floor. At last she decided that as the eldest, it was probably her responsibility. Taking a deep breath, she stepped forward and raised her arm. It had been an automatic gesture, lifting her arm for permission to speak, as if she was back in school. However, instead of soothing Papa it appeared to irritate him.

"So, so I am a tyrant in your eyes. You even stand at attention like wooden soldiers. And you, my Liseleh? You're afraid of me too. Very well, if you think I'm a general then I will act like one. What is it, Private Stein?"

Lisa was momentarily wordless. "Well you see, sir, I mean, Papa, we didn't mean that you are a dictator . . . I mean we don't know whether you are one or not. Oh dear, that is, none of us know who Ghengis Khan or Ras . . . Rasputin is it, are anyway, so we couldn't answer you yes or no."

Her reply seemed to make Papa happier. Lisa almost thought she glimpsed a slight tremor at the corner of his mouth but Papa again began circling the room.

"I see, North American schools are so bad that they don't even teach children world history. Not like my gymnasium in the old country. Your mother is right. This is an inferior school and we'll have to get you away from here."

Lisa had said something wrong and she didn't know what it was. Now they had another problem. Papa was going to move them to another town, smaller still she supposed, and all because of that Rasputin man.

"Rasputin was a terribly cruel and vicious man who

lived at the time of the last Russian Czar. All the people were frightened stiff of this insane man . . ." Papa began. He then proceeded to tell them all about Rasputin and Ghengis Khan. When Papa was in the right mood he really did tell the best stories in the world. But now? Still standing at attention they listened to him for fifteen minutes. The phone broke the spell and Papa glanced at his watch.

"Oh my, the store. I must go."

"Papa, you're not really a Rasputin," Suzanne said.

"That was a great story, Papa, but what are you going to do to us?"

Lisa, Teddy and Suzanne all glared at Mike. Since Papa had forgotten the purpose of this conversation, why not leave the subject alone?

"That is the number one question. You have been liars, you have been deceitful and you have wasted your time on this acting business when you knew I do not approve of such nonsense. Above all, in keeping secrets from Mama and me, you show you do not respect us."

"Okay, okay, haven't you scolded us enough already? What happens to our puppets?" replied Teddy.

"Always with his backtalk. That's quite enough, young man. A rebel I have. Be quiet, you hear."

If only Teddy had bitten his tongue. Lisa watched Papa's ears turn pink and the flush spread over his face. Oh, it seemed that they almost had begun to understand Papa and then this had to happen.

"That's it in a nutshell, you hear. Yes, I spoke to your Mrs. Beddlington about your shenanigans this morning. She phoned to congratulate you. Said you'd also won some popularity award. She asked that I please try to have a little

pity and understanding for 'such talented children!'"
Papa became vicious as he imitated the teacher.

"No more monkey business, do you hear? A dictator you
think I am. Well then, I shall show you how a dictator acts.
Having a teacher plead for her poor lambs. You can keep
those blasted puppets but not in the house anymore."

"But Irving, the chicken coop you mentioned," Mama
interrupted from the doorway.

He scowled at her. "Yes, out of the house. You can keep
them in the old deserted chicken coop behind the store
. . . across the back lane here. It's warm now that spring
is here, more air there too, and who knows what winter
will bring? I insist that all of you complete every single
chore each day before you go near the puppets. And you
keep out of my way, young man, hear?" he said, looking at
Teddy.

Within a week they had moved all their puppets and
stage equipment down to the chicken coop. It really was a
wonderful old building. A perfect place. It had a strange
slanted roof that was high in the front and swept lower at
the back like a big slide. It was great for jumping competi-
tions. There were a few windows on the lane side of the
building although several panes of glass had become
shattered. It took a long time to clean up the place but it
was worth it when they completed the job.

All their friends, impressed with the success of the
puppet show, were delighted to assist them with their
work. Ben had proved almost as talented as Tom in repair-
ing things. Unfortunately, he had returned to the city for
the final term of school.

They had blocked out the drafts creeping in the broken

windows by using heavy corrugated cardboard and tar paper. The girls swept out the accumulation of straw, cobwebs and chicken droppings while the boys carted away junk. They also built rough tables and shelves for the puppets. There was plenty of room for the stage since only part of the coop was used to store wood and old crates. Some of the puppets were settled on specially labeled shelves, while the most valuable ones were stored in a huge antique chest Mama had given them.

Shortly after Ben's departure, a letter arrived from one of the judges inviting them to take part in a stage show in the city in the autumn.

"Hey, isn't that great? Boy, will that be exciting," Lisa said as she shared the letter with the gang. They were all seated, dusting the dolls. They constantly improved their puppets, making new characters for their plays and cleaning them when not in use. They seldom put on shows now that it was spring, but they still worked on the dolls.

"Sure, sure, if you get the old man to go along with it," Teddy replied.

Suzanne, who was wiping a table by the window, motioned for silence. She pointed out that Papa and Mama were coming across the lane from the store to inspect the new place.

This time they did not dare mention their hopes as Papa and Mama walked around the place. Papa even examined the shelves for dirt and gave a pleasant nod as he saw how the puppets were labeled. Mike showed him the big wooden chest where their special treasures were kept.

"It still needs a coat of oil to really look good."

"So, you can really be responsible?"

"Teddy did most of the work," Lisa replied.

"Glad to hear he can assume some responsibility, because he's going to have a lot more when you leave."

"What do you mean, Papa?"

"Why, when you go to private school in Edmonton this fall," Papa replied. Lisa shook her head in bewilderment.

"Lisa, dear, you forgot that the school here doesn't go past grade eight," Mama said gently.

"But some of the other kids will go to the nearest large town by bus to their high school. Why can't I do that?"

"Because I want you to have the best education so you can do something with yourself," Papa replied. "That means boarding school in a city, not shilly-shallying around here with puppets and acting and all the other imaginary poppycock. Being with more children your age."

"But I don't want to be alone in the city. I want to be here with my family." Lisa allowed the tears to stream down her face.

"If Lisa goes, I go too," Teddy shouted.

Mama put her arms around her two oldest children and Papa stormed to the door.

"And I say it is already settled. And that is that." He turned to face the children glaring at him. He moved slowly out the door and the bounce was missing from his usual walk. At that moment he looked much older than in the past.

13

Yet Another Adventure

WHAT AN UNBELIEVABLY TERRIBLE period the last two weeks of August had been — like a nightmare. Why had their parents spoiled the whole year in Chatko Falls by deciding to send her to school in Edmonton? Lisa just shook her head again as she stood wavering atop a kitchen chair.

She peered down at Mama, crouched on her knees on the linoleum floor below the chair. Dimly, she was aware of a muffled voice telling her to stop slouching and to stand still. She pushed back her shoulders — might as well become accustomed to doing things in a military manner; after all the New Alberta School of Education for Young Ladies was probably full of grumpy old teachers who would constantly be telling her to improve her posture. She stuck her tummy out as far as it would go, and imagined an old maid with a tight bun at the back of her head, chiding her for her terrible posture. What if she stuck out her tongue at the teacher? Maybe they would send her back to her family.

"Lisa Stein, stop that wiggling. Your hem is going to look like a wavy ocean if you move once more. Always daydreaming, and with only a day to finish all these uniforms."

Lucky that Mama had remembered to take the pins out of her mouth before she spoke this time. "What if I disgrace you, Mama? What if I'm an awful student . . . after all, I've attended twelve different schools since I began grade one, and what if I break some golden rule and am expelled . . . what will you do then, eh?"

"Hmm, talking rubbish again. Knew you were daydreaming. Let's not have any cheeky talk like that, young lady."

"Would you maybe put me in a girls' reformatory?"

"You will not be expelled. No child of Papa's would ever be expelled and besides the headmistress said you were perfect material for the new school. Intelligent and well-bred were her words." Mama looked up from the hem she was still pinning and gave Lisa a very unusual impish smile.

"Maybe she meant by perfect material that I really needed the atmosphere of that jail." All of them called it the jail. They knew that it irritated Papa. Although he pretended not to hear them, you could see the tips of his earlobes going pink and his bald spot turning color. "All I know is that in the *Emily Goes Away to School* series all the girls were constantly trying to escape. . . ."

"From what, Liseleh? From the lovely classrooms, from the fine uniforms, from the superior education? They must have been very light-headed girls to begin with, or else it was a different kind of school."

"Wish I could have a new wardrobe like you, Lisa," Suzanne called from her bedroom. Always eavesdropping. "A whole set of new blouses, and a gym outfit, and three navy uniforms, and a navy coat and hat and even a blazer. Here I have to stay home and do all your extra chores and you get to be part of the fascinating world."

Suzanne never could resist the temptation to dramatize. She had complained that she too should be released from this little town but when Lisa had offered to change places with her, Papa had thumped the table and said one daughter absent from home was enough.

"Green blazers, icky . . . green blazer with the silly school emblem and with navy uniform . . . horrible . . . and black stockings."

"Well, it's too bad you have straight hair since they won't let you curl it anyway — now me . . ."

Mama had finished the pinning and Lisa jumped down. "Go finish packing your trunk," Mama advised. Only two more days. As she turned to go to her room Lisa noticed how exhausted Mama seemed. Her graying hair hung in untidy wisps around her face. Mama usually looked so neat. Lisa couldn't resist brushing back a lock of Mama's fine hair. She was really going to miss Mama, though certainly not Papa. Teddy had been right all along. Papa didn't care about them.

"Lisa," Mama said, kissing her forehead in a gesture that Lisa remembered from her baby days, "I'm going to miss my big daughter. Not only because you've been such a big help to me in the house and in the store, but because you're such a happy, sensible girl." Then Mama turned quickly away and Lisa saw the tears glimmering on her cheeks. "Now shoo, go finish packing."

It was an hour before she finally had a moment to find Teddy. He had been so morose lately that Lisa was worried. What would happen to Teddy without her to calm him down? He hadn't spoken a word to Papa since the day their father had made the announcement about her move to Edmonton. She knew he would be in the chicken coop with the puppets, and she found him lying on his stomach on an old blanket in the corner. While the place smelled of new paint he was absorbed in a book.

"Good book, Teddy? I wasn't able to come out until Mama finished that silly pinning business."

At first he appeared not to have heard her. When he finally rolled over on his back, he had a fiery scowl on his face. "I'm planning my trip, too. This book tells you how to get into the merchant marines. They don't ask any questions about your age and you can sail all over the world."

"Oh, Teddy, you wouldn't do a thing like that to Mama. Now she needs you more than ever."

He appeared unmoved by her words. "At first I thought of the French Foreign Legion, where every man has a hidden past and takes a new name, but that was childish. How could I ever hope to scrape together enough money to get to Africa? No, the Canadian merchant ships are the best. I'll hitchhike to the west coast."

She didn't want to hurt Teddy's feelings, but this really had gone too far. "Oh, Teddy, you sound like a character from Jack London. It isn't so easy to go to sea anymore. And besides, what if you got sick — like yellow fever — in a foreign port, or got tired of seeing the world . . . you couldn't just change your mind and come back home. Why, on ships the captain is the ruler and he could keel-haul you or something dreadful like that."

Even Teddy laughed at her reference to keel-hauling. "And now who's pulling a Suzanne? Don't think I'd have any problems with so many ports. After all, Papa moves us constantly. Bet the ocean is full of sailors who have tyrants for fathers."

"But I'd never see you again for years, and you'd have a long beard and maybe I wouldn't even recognize you and besides," she thought quickly, "who'd take care of the puppets?"

"Ah, they're kid stuff. Who cares about a bunch of old wooden puppets now? I've made up my mind and the day after you leave, I go too, with this." He pointed to his thumb. "Look, you've got one day left. Let's go outside and enjoy it."

That evening, after she had closed her trunk, and pulled her plump comforter tightly around her chin, she was unable to sleep. She wondered if she should talk to Mama about Teddy. But Mama was bound to tell Papa and then Teddy never'd confide in her again. But how to approach Papa? She mapped out conversations several times, but they always ended up the wrong way. Papa laughed or Papa became angry with Teddy and locked him up or took away his privileges. She pulled the heavy comforter tighter around her face. She was going to miss it. What if they only used blankets instead of the old eiderdowns? How could she sleep? No, if she spoke to Papa something dreadful was sure to happen. Teddy would never trust her again. Besides, they'd be sure to catch Teddy on the road anyway. But what if they didn't, and some horrible tramps kidnapped him? She drifted off into a troubled sleep and woke much later with a start. She had just dreamed of a nasty captain hitting Teddy with his cat-o'-nine-tails. She was unable to go back to sleep and, pulling on her bathrobe, walked to the kitchen for some milk.

Carrying her glass and tiptoeing so she would not waken the family she walked down the back hall. As a boarder at the school she'd never feel free to go to the icebox in the middle of the night. She stared vacantly through the window. The town was absolutely still this muggy night. Indian summer was so beautiful in the country. The leaves turning copper and gold and ruby-colored. She'd miss all that. She took one last glance through the window. There was a flicker of red down below in the direction of the chicken coop. An alley cat? No, their eyes weren't that big. Someone prowling around with a flashlight? A sudden premonition brought goose pimples to her arms and she squinted her eyes, to take a better look. It wasn't a flashlight. It was a flame, a quavering flame stroking the roof. For a moment she was spellbound. Then the glass clattered to the floor, smashing on the linoleum. She rushed back down the hall, shouting.

"Wake up, everyone, wake up quickly. The chicken coop is on fire. Teddy, Papa, Mama, Mike!" Fearfully she hammered on their doors. For the first time in her life she threw open her parents' door without knocking and flicked on the light switch.

"Papa, come quick. The chicken coop is on fire. Call the firemen, get help." Both Papa and Mama sat up like a pair of jack-in-the-boxes. Papa looked strange without his thick glasses and he bolted from the bed, only pausing to pull a robe over his red flannel nightshirt.

She bumped into Teddy running down the hall. "Oh, Teddy, the puppets, come quick, quickly." And as she watched in stunned silence, more flames gulped at the dry shingles.

"Oh, Lisa, is it bad? Our puppets, we must save our puppets." Together they rushed down the outside staircase with Papa and the others right at their heels. By the time they were in the alley the flames had covered half the roof and Lisa could see them licking at the back of the building. Smoke was gushing from the broken window.

"Good girl, Lisa, lucky you saw it," Papa said. "It might even spread across to the store. Start pouring water." And Papa headed toward the store.

Moments later, as they stood pumping from their well, they heard the shrill ring of the burglar alarm in the store. Papa had chosen the fastest method of alerting the townspeople. Mama followed Suzanne and Mike hauling buckets, metal tubs and even the dishpan.

"Quick, let's make a bucket brigade," Teddy directed. More people arrived to see what the commotion was and they joined the ever-growing line from the pump to the coop. Two husky men took turns manning the pump and all the others passed down the sloshing pails of water.

Nothing seemed to contain the fire. Finally two galloping horses pulling the fire wagon drew up to the lane. By this time a slight wind was fanning the snaking flames in several directions. Thick gobs of black smoke billowed from the broken windows and seeped under the roof. "Lisa, there's no time. Come quick and get the puppets," Teddy screamed frantically. "They'll die . . . be burned to a crisp. Frizzled."

"But Teddy, there's fire inside too. We'd get hurt. The firemen will control the blaze."

Suddenly, like a sizzling pan of fat on the stove, the fire would no longer be contained and it erupted with a *poof* that shook the building.

Teddy shouted for his puppets and at the same time they heard one of the firemen calling, "Just try to keep it from jumping across the alley to the stores. It's too late to save this building, fellows."

"You see, we've got to save them ourselves . . . our friends . . . can't desert them," her brother roared in desperation. "Get as near the door as you can and I'll throw them out."

"Oh, Teddy, I want to save the puppets as much as you do but the roof will cave in, just look at it. And then what will happen to you?" They both looked up to see that there was a new flame crackling from the roof. Teddy shook his head and hurtled past the crowd of people toward the door. He pushed the handle but the door refused to budge. Finally he ran at it and hit it hard with his shoulder. The door flew open.

"Come here, you rascal. Trying to get yourself killed? The roof is going to fall in soon." Papa had rushed after Teddy as he entered the doorway and was holding the struggling boy by the collar of his shirt. Teddy's feet barely touched the ground. "Now get back there before I throw you there," he barked.

Then Papa did a peculiar thing. Having pushed Teddy into the arms of one of the men, he grabbed a coat from another, sloshed it in a nearby pail of water, and threw it over himself.

"If I'm not out in three minutes, come and get me," he shouted. Then Papa vanished through the door of the chicken coop. Everyone gasped. Lisa looked at the struggling Teddy and he shook his head in bewilderment. The silence that followed Papa's disappearance into the building was funereal. Perhaps, like Lisa, everyone felt that if they held their breath the roof would remain intact.

Just as the head fireman was motioning for the others to move forward, Papa appeared at the door, dragging their huge trunk of puppets. He pushed it through the door, disappeared again like a genie in the smoke and then emerged carrying a heap of puppets in his arms. As he stopped to catch his breath outside the doorway there was a rumble and with a gigantic shiver the roof collapsed into the coop.

All of them moved back as the sparks flew in every direction. Lisa didn't remember what followed. It was all one great turmoil. She saw Teddy moving toward Papa with his right hand proffered, as if he was going to give Papa a handshake, but he appeared to change his mind and instead ran into Papa's arms; and Papa, allowing the sopping coat to slip off his shoulders, embraced Teddy.

Despite the noise of the firemen barking orders about controlling the flames, she managed to hear Teddy call to Papa. "You did care, you really do care. You saved our puppets."

An hour later they were all drinking hot chocolate around the kitchen table. The chicken coop was a smoldering wreck but no other buildings had been damaged. In the middle of the room was the chest of precious puppets. Teddy was gently cleaning soot off the face of the giant while Lisa shook black flakes off the clothes of the dolls.

Papa touched the surface of the antique chest and shook his head. "For once, it's a shame that you were such good housekeepers," he said.

"What do you mean, Irving?" Mama asked.

"The firemen found a charred linseed oil bottle in the cinders. They wondered if you left the oily cloths you were using in the chicken coop?"

The children nodded. "Sure, yesterday we finally oiled the chest and did some painting. Then we just dropped the rags in a box with the other trash for —"

"Never studied spontaneous combustion in school?" Papa interrupted. "Well, that probably explains how the fire started — when the rags began smoldering — but we'll never know for certain."

"At least she's safe; the ballerina's skirt isn't even singed," Lisa replied as she pulled her favorite from the pile of marionettes.

Lisa brought the dainty dancer over to Papa. "She is very special. An actor at the Pantages Theatre gave her to us."

"She is lovely, Lisa. Sorry I didn't have time to save any more."

"But Papa, we have most of them and the others won't be hard to duplicate and if it wasn't for you —" Papa stopped Teddy.

"Papa, you're a hero," Mike pronounced.

"Oh, Mama, weren't you proud of Papa?"

Hesitantly, Lisa turned to her father. "You really did care about our puppet theater all the time, but why didn't you ever tell us before?"

"Now all we have to do is build a new puppet theater," Teddy said.

"Well maybe you should wait for a while," Papa said slowly. "Be hard to transport, and besides, this time it should be a really professional theater."

"And Papa's just the man to help you," Mama said.

They all stared at Papa. It was still difficult to imagine that their solemn Papa had ever been interested in the theater. But then tonight had been full of strange happenings. Obviously adults also kept secrets from their children. Lisa tried to understand this and then decided it was too complicated. It was a pity grownups had such strange ways. They certainly kept their children guessing. But Teddy was looking at Papa with such pride.

"For he's a jolly good fellow, for he's . . ." Suzanne started to sing. They all joined in. But something was still missing. Lisa tried to think what was bothering her — something had been said.

When they finally concluded the song she remembered. "Papa, what did you mean when you said the puppet theater might be hard to transport — to where? To the house?"

"Esther, I'm sure now. Maybe you were right," Papa replied, adding yet another riddle to the evening.

"What are you talking about, Irving? I don't understand either."

"Why, moving to Edmonton, of course. Your uncle told me of a store there, could really be good, and Putnam's been pestering me to sell this place to him for a few months now. Of course, it would mean you'd have to leave all your friends here, children, and move again in another month — you know, new schools, new house, all that stuff you hate." He gave them all a sober look but his eyes were twinkling. "I leave the final decision to Mama."

Nobody waited for him to conclude. They knew that Papa always made the final decisions. They dashed toward him but Mama was there first.

"Really, Irving, a city finally, really? Are you sure you can manage it?" Papa nodded.

"When do we leave?" Mama asked, with no hesitancy. "I must start packing."

"Why, then I'd be able to live with my family, my wonderful, crazy family. We'd all be together and the puppets too." Lisa didn't know whom to embrace first. So she grabbed the ballerina doll with one hand and threw the other arm over Teddy's shoulders. Even her new school might be fun now. And maybe, just maybe, someday there'd even be a white house with a huge veranda and apple trees. After all, with Papa moving them so often, they were bound to encounter such a house someday, somewhere.